DESTI[
IN
TENERIfE

DESTINY
IN
TENERIFE

Evelyn Hood

This first world edition published in Great Britain 2000 by
SEVERN HOUSE PUBLISHERS LTD of
9–15 High Street, Sutton, Surrey SM1 1DF.
This first world edition published in the USA 2000 by
SEVERN HOUSE PUBLISHERS INC of
595 Madison Avenue, New York, N.Y. 10022.

British Library Cataloguing in Publication Data

Hood, Evelyn, 1936-
    Destiny in Tenerife
    1.   Love stories
    I.   Title
    823.9'14 [F]

    ISBN 0-7278-5566-2

Typeset by Palimpsest Book Production Ltd.,
Polmont, Stirlingshire, Scotland.
Printed and bound in Great Britain by
MPG Books Ltd, Bodmin, Cornwall.

One

R ain rattled at the windows with agitated fingertips and the wind hurled itself across the wide, shallow valley to batter against the grey stone walls of the house.

The doors and windows were all locked against the stormy night, the fire glowed and the kitchen was softly lit by a few candles that Morrin had found in the cupboard when the lights first went out. The room was cosy and all she had to do, she told herself as the trees in the garden croaked and rustled ominously, was sit tight and wait. The storm would pass, and if the worst came to the worst she could always spend the night in Mrs Plover's comfortable armchair by the fire.

She wished that the elderly housekeeper hadn't decided to visit her new grandchild on that particular day, but when Mrs Plover went off to catch her bus, overnight bag in hand, there had been no storm and Morrin hadn't intended to work so late.

Normally the house was filled with noise – the dogs barking, the phone ringing, Mrs Plover singing in the kitchen, Gareth's presence crackling through every room.

Now, with the place silent and the wind moaning outside, Morrin was so nervous that even her own reflection in the dark window as she filled the kettle was enough to make her jump. Setting the kettle hurriedly on the gas cooker, she went back to pull the curtains closed, then paused, staring at her reflection in the dark glass. Candlelight brushed her long, softly curling hair with gold, framing her oval face softly and giving her usually serious dark blue eyes a sparkle. For a moment she looked, then twitched the curtains together, saying aloud, "Don't get any ideas, my girl . . . you're very ordinary when the electric light's working!"

The sound of her own voice was cheering, but as she went back to her seat by the fire silence crowded in on her again. It was her own fault . . . she shouldn't have decided to type the final chapters of her employer's latest novel before driving back to her bedsit in the nearby town. But with Gareth and Mrs Plover both away for the night there had been nobody to remind her of the time, and she had worked on, unaware of the approaching storm until sudden, strong gusts of wind slammed against the sturdy stone house, the computer screen went blank, and the lights flickered and died. It was only then that she realised how lonely the house was, with its nearest neighbours almost a quarter of a mile away.

In the few months since she had started working for Gareth Sinclair, Morrin had come to love his home in the Yorkshire Dales, a solid stone two-storey structure built into a wooded hillside with large front windows overlooking the valley below and the magnificent sweep of hills opposite. There was only one problem – as well as loving the house, she had come to love its owner with a passion that could never, ever, be resolved, for she was not the sort of woman who appealed to Gareth Sinclair.

It was part of Morrin's job as Gareth's secretary to book tables in the best restaurants, organise cosy weekends for two, and order flowers for these escorts who, like Sinclair himself, were cool and sophisticated, adult enough to indulge in affairs then say goodbye gracefully when the time came, as it always did.

It hurt, being a conventional love-and-marriage person in love with someone like that. In her fantasies Morrin pictured herself dining and dancing with him, sharing a secluded hotel room with him – but her dreams always floundered then foundered when it came to the sophisticated goodbye. Gareth wasn't a forever man.

Wrenching her mind away from the yearning that only depressed her, Morrin heard rain spattering against the curtained windows and the boom of the wind rushing across the valley to throw itself against the back of the house. As it retreated, thwarted, the trees sighed and bushes near the back door shushed them nervously.

All at once the sturdy, safe stone walls of the house seemed to be a prison, trapping her within its depths. If only Gareth hadn't taken the dogs with him, if only . . .

"Oh, stop moaning," she said aloud, half to herself and half to the wind. She reached for the little transistor radio Mrs Plover kept on the window sill, then froze. Above the noise of the storm she could hear

3

another sound, a scratching and scuffling from the big front hall.

She swallowed her fear, fingers tight against her mouth. She could jam a chair beneath the front door knob, she thought, though it was probably just a window rattling anyway. Then, realising that her fear of the unknown was worse than anything she might have to face in real life, she picked up the heavy hearth poker and eased herself silently through the kitchen door.

As she inched her way through the dark hall, trying to remember where its few pieces of furniture were situated, the noise came again. This time there was no mistaking the sound of someone trying to get in through the front door. Morrin's mind worked frantically, but it was difficult to work out a plan when her heart was hammering against her ribs and the breath was catching in her throat.

There was a telephone in Gareth's study and another in the sitting-room, but none in the hall. She was trying to decide which phone was the nearest, and wondering if they were still working, when the door crashed back on its hinges and a gust of wind surged in. Morrin scarcely had time to register its icy touch on her cheek before the hall was filled with movement and panting and the skitter of claws against the parquet flooring. The poker flew from her hand as a muscular tail whipped against her legs. As it clattered to the floor a torch beam flicked on and found her.

"Who the . . . Morrin? Polly, Daniel – get out of the way!" Gareth Sinclair roared, then, as the dogs obeyed, "What on earth are you doing here at this time of night?"

"Oh Gareth, thank goodness it's only you!" She flew to him, clutching at the sleeve of his wet coat for comfort.

"Well now. Mrs P never throws herself into my arms when I come home to her. I could grow to like this, with a little encouragement," Gareth said, sliding his arm about her with an ease born of years of practice. For a luxurious moment she allowed herself to relax against him, then common sense jangled alarm bells through her mind and she pulled back. As far as girls like Morrin were concerned, men like Gareth Sinclair wore 'Don't Touch!' notices.

He gave a dramatic sigh. "I thought it was too good to be true. Where did we go wrong?"

"The lights have all gone out – the storm—" As he released her she tugged her sweater straight and smoothed her skirt.

"So I gathered as I drove along the road. Not a light to be seen anywhere. Hang on," he said as rain spattered through the open doorway on to the polished wooden floor.

Once the door was closed, the storm, denied entry, beat sullenly against the walls and rattled at the letter box for admission. Gareth, ignoring it, returned to Morrin.

"What are you doing here at this hour? Where's Mrs P? Don't we have cand— Good Lord, what's that doing there?" he interrupted himself as the torch beam teased an answering gleam from the heavy ornamental poker.

"So that's what caused all the noise? You weren't really going to hit me with it, were you?" There was a note of awe in his voice.

"I thought you were a burglar." She rushed to justify herself. "You weren't supposed to be coming back tonight and I was alone with all the lights out—"

"I decided that a long drive was better than spending the night as my brother's guest." He picked up the poker. Even in his large hand it looked menacingly heavy. "Do you realise the damage you could have done with this? And don't bother explaining anything until we've got some light – and some food."

"There are candles in the kitchen," she volunteered, and the torch was thrust into her hand.

"You take that and I'll keep the poker. I feel safer that way," said Gareth. "Lead on."

In the kitchen the two dogs, an Old English sheepdog and a black poodle, were already settled before the fire. Gareth took off his coat, dropped it on to a chair, and ran a hand through his storm-tossed hair. "Sit down," he commanded, then, as Morrin sank into Mrs Plover's chair, "Where's Mrs P – and why are you here at this time of night? Begin at the beginning."

Her earlier fears seemed ridiculous now that he was here, filling the house with life, making it friendly and safe again. As she explained the housekeeper's absence he unbuttoned his pale grey suit jacket, pulled off the green tie that matched his eyes and opened the top button of his white shirt. Gareth hated formal clothes.

"You idiot," he said in the indulgent older-brother

voice that made her squirm. "Didn't you see the storm coming?"

"I was too busy."

His shoulders rose and fell in a shrug. "I don't know – most secretaries go off on a spree when they're left on their own, but not you. I thought you'd have wanted to go shopping or get your hair done or meet someone. That's what most women like to do, isn't it?"

The implication that she was like his empty-headed girlfriends stung a sharp note into her answer. "I'm not most women. And your book's supposed to be finished and sent to the publisher this week."

"It will be," he said easily. "Still plenty of time. What would you have done if I hadn't decided to come home tonight?"

"I'd have spent the night in here." She felt more foolish by the minute, especially when he threw his head back and laughed.

"Oh yes? Curled up in a chair with the poker clutched in your little fist? Lucky for the burglars that I came home when I did," he said, then, "Can you cook as efficiently as you can type?"

"As long as you don't want anything elaborate."

"Good. We'll eat in the sitting-room and let those two have this fire." He nudged the dogs with the toe of his polished shoe and the sheepdog raised his head, yawned, thumped his tail on the carpet, and settled down again.

"Lazy beasts," Gareth said affectionately, and picked up his torch. "I'll find more candles and get changed. By the way—" He turned at the door and grinned, his green eyes mocking her in the candlelight, "If you think you hear intruders just scream and let me deal with them. I don't want you to go splashing their blood all over the house."

Camilla, Morrin thought with resentment as she gathered eggs and cheese and milk and butter together, wouldn't have made an idiot of herself. Camilla, a leggy, lovely blonde, was Gareth's current escort. Whipping eggs into a froth, she decided smugly that Camilla probably couldn't even boil water.

"I found plenty of candles," Gareth said cheerfully from behind her.

"Does Camilla cook?" Morrin asked without thinking, then blushed.

"Like a dream; she took some special course in Paris. What made you ask?"

"She phoned today – several times." It had only been twice.

"Why?"

Morrin began to grate cheese. "I don't know. She wants you to call back."

"She can wait until tomorrow. Right now I'm hungry. What still needs doing?"

Setting him to making the toast, Morrin thought to herself that Gareth's indifference to his latest girlfriend's phone calls was a clear indication that whether she knew it or not, Camilla was on her way out of his life.

When the food was ready he led the way into the living-room, carrying a loaded tray. He had already coaxed the fire into a blaze and arranged candles so that the hearth rug, one sofa and a chair were in a pool of golden light, with the rest of the room in shadow. Setting the tray down on a coffee table before the fire he dropped to the rug, propping his shoulders against the sofa, and proceeded to open a bottle of wine. He had towelled his damp hair and left it to curl about his face, and had changed into a bulky black sweater and jeans.

Morrin, unused to being alone with her employer in such an informal setting, perched on the edge of the armchair. "How did your meeting go?"

He wrinkled his nose. "Same as always. Brother Tom reported on t'mill, sister Kate tried to argue with him on every point that was raised, and I signed a few things. Try this." He handed her a glass of wine.

Gareth always referred to the family business as 't'mill' and he always, when speaking about it, lapsed into a Yorkshire dialect, though years in boarding school had left him with only a faint touch of the Dales where he had grown up and still lived. He and his sister were sleeping partners in the business, which was controlled by an older brother who had worked his way up through every department.

Morrin sipped at the wine. "It's nice," she ventured, then flushed as Gareth said, "I'm glad that moddom approves. It's one of my best bottles."

"No sense in wasting it on me, then," she said defensively. "I hardly ever drink wine."

"If you like it, it's not wasted," he told her briskly.

As they ate, the wind continued to moan outside, but to Morrin it had lost its mournful wail, and the tapping

9

of the rain's skeletal fingers on the windows sounded almost cheerful now that Gareth was there.

"Drink up," he urged. "I'm not going to empty this bottle on my own."

"One's enough when I'm driving."

"You're not driving, not in this weather and at this time of night. I switched on the gas fire in the spare room while I was upstairs."

"Oh," she said, startled. "But I can't possibly—"

"Yes you can. Your little car would be blown off the road in this storm, or you'd be hit by a falling tree. You were already planning to stay overnight anyway, weren't you?" Then he looked up at her from where he sprawled on the floor, and grinned. "Things are different now that I'm here, is that it? Tell you what, Morrin – I won't molest you if you promise not to molest me."

Her face burned. "I didn't – I wasn't—"

"Don't panic." He poured more wine into both glasses. "It's against my principles to force myself on you of all people. I can't afford to lose a good secretary. Mind you" – he pushed his empty place aside and stretched his long legs across the rug – "most women would feel offended if I didn't make some attempt to seduce them. What makes you so different?"

"I'll make coffee," Morrin said hurriedly and leaned forward to pick up the plates. His hand closed on hers.

"Running away again. When are you going to grow up, Morrin?"

"I am grown up!"

10

"What age are you now? Eighteen, going on forty-two?" he teased, and laughed when she pulled her hand free and scurried to the kitchen.

From their first meeting he had been intrigued by her age. To Gareth, any female below twenty-two years was a mere child. He couldn't get over the fact that at eighteen years of age Morrin was a trained and efficient secretary. All the women in his life were either comfortably off or made a great deal of money through their looks, as models. Camilla – who was dominating Morrin's thoughts in a very irritating way that night – was the spoiled daughter of a wealthy man.

As she made coffee Morrin wondered who was going to take Camilla's place. She had grown to hate the first weeks of each new affair; the intimate phone calls, the preoccupation that meant that his mind was elsewhere. Now she was going to have to go through it again.

He was pouring brandy into balloon glasses when she went back into the sitting-room. "I thought we'd do things in style. After all, this is our first dinner together," he said casually, then, nodding at the sturdy coffee mugs in her hands, "This is the first restaurant that's known how to serve coffee properly. I hate those tiny cups they usually hand out."

As he leaned forward to poke the fire into a blaze the leaping flames danced in the depths of his eyes, emphasising his high cheekbones and strong humorous mouth. His face was a little too broad, his nose a little too long for the faultless good looks of a film star. But those compelling eyes, the thick black hair and expressive features made him incredibly attractive.

Then he moved back from the fire and his face was hidden from her as he settled down, his back against her chair. At first she was keenly aware that his shoulder was warm and solid against her leg, then as he began to talk about the meeting he had attended she found herself relaxing, answering him easily, laughing with him. The firelight, the cosiness of the candlelit room, the sharp, pleasant tang of the brandy on her tongue, the security of knowing that she was no longer alone – all these things combined to overcome her initial awkwardness.

Up until tonight she had taken care to keep their relationship on strictly formal lines. From the first, his casual teasing attitude towards her had invited her to treat him as a friend, or even an older brother, rather than an employer, but she had denied herself that pleasure. An only child raised by shy parents, she had never found it easy to make friends of either sex, but with Gareth it was even more difficult. Almost from the beginning she had found him disturbing: at first she thought that there was something unlikeable about him, although she could not identify it. She was totally in love with him before she realised what was happening to her.

Therein lay the danger – she could not allow herself to love him. She must remain as an impersonal part of his life. He would be appalled if he sensed the truth. Worse, he would be amused and then irritated, and she couldn't bear that.

It had not been easy to maintain her cool aloof manner

but she had worked hard at it, needing it for protection. But now, with firelight and candlelight lapping them in a charmed circle of gold and Gareth's shoulder warm against her leg, she let her guard slip, talking about her parents, her home in the south-west, her college days.

"And what about the man in your life?" he asked lazily as she leaned forward to put her empty mug on the coffee table.

"There isn't one."

"Come on – there must be someone, somewhere." He twisted to face her, his green eyes, points of light dancing deep within them, travelling over her face. "Don't tell me" – his voice dropped to a teasing murmur – "that you've reached the grand old age of eighteen and never been kissed?"

"That is none of—"

"—my business," he finished for her, reaching for her hand and trapping it in his before she had time to draw it away. Turning it over in his he opened her curled fingers gently, one by one. A shiver ran through Morrin's body at his touch.

"Gareth—" She meant to speak sharply, to snatch her hand away, but her voice was a whisper.

"What?" His free hand stretched up to touch the long hair shadowing her down-turned face, fingers curling about a thick strand then tightening and tugging gently.

For a split second the alarm bells sounded in her head, then the clamour receded, dulled by Gareth's touch. It seemed natural to let herself slip from the chair into his arms and to feel, at last, his lips on hers.

13

Two

G areth's kiss was gentle and yet it flamed through Morrin with an intensity that made her body quiver. She had wondered, from their first meeting, what it would be like to be held in his arms. Now she knew, and she didn't ever want the magic moment to stop.

When his mouth left hers her eyes fluttered open and she parted her lips in a soft sigh.

"Funny," he said, "I could have sworn that by this time you would have tried to slap my face. You're entitled to one slap." She reached up to touch his face. "Well," he murmured, "you've had your chance," and bent to claim her lips again, before travelling with tantalising slowness down her throat to rest on the soft skin at the neck of her blue sweater. As she arched her head back to expose her throat to his kisses part of Morrin's mind, the practical part, was shocked by her behaviour, but it was only a token protest, quickly smothered, as his mouth warmed her breasts through the thin woollen sweater and she buried her face in his hair, inhaling its outdoor fragrance, by the pleasure of being with him at last.

Freeing one arm, Gareth pulled a cushion from the

14

chair where she had been sitting and tossed it to the rug before easing her down to lie with her head pillowed. As he leaned over her firelight danced over the planes and angles of his face. She reached up to touch him, but he took her hands in one of his, kissing the fingertips. Morrin sighed again, closing her eyes, smiling as she felt one finger gently tracing the outline of her face, stroking a curl back from her forehead. He touched the upturned corners of her mouth and said, "Why have you kept it a secret for so long?"

"Kept what a secret?"

"All this passion. I like it," he murmured, then suddenly the room beyond his head flared into harsh, revealing light.

Morrin's hands flew instinctively to cover her eyes, then she took them away as she heard Gareth say, "And then there was light . . . just at the wrong time, too. Well, we can fix that."

"No . . ." She sat up as he scrambled to his feet. Shame swept over her as she looked round the bright room, seeing the empty dishes and glasses on the table, the cushion on the floor, her own dishevelled appearance. "Leave it on!"

Her hair was a mess, her skirt tangled round her thighs, her sweater rumpled up. She got up, frantically trying to tidy herself. "We mustn't – I mean, I'm sorry . . . I should never have . . ."

Her voice was panicky, and so were her movements as she smoothed her hair with shaking hands and replaced the cushion on the chair, averting her face from him.

"What's all the panic about?" His voice took on an edge. "We're adults, both free to follow our inclinations. And I must say, I like your inclinations. So what's wrong? Relax, Morrin, enjoy life."

"It was a . . . a mistake, that's all. We shouldn't have—" She was babbling like an idiot but she couldn't stop her tongue from running on. She scurried about the room, blowing out the candles and gathering the dishes together. "Where's the tray?"

"It's a bit late to say that we shouldn't have." Gareth came back to her, catching her by the shoulders and turning her about to face him. "Because we did, didn't we? And I for one enjoyed it."

Unable to meet his gaze she concentrated instead on staring at his chin. But that meant that she could also see the warm, passionate mouth that had so easily aroused her answering desire. Far too easily. She closed her eyes.

"Don't tell me you weren't having a good time as well. I had no idea that a quiet little scrap of a thing like you could be so . . ."

"Stop it!" She tried to twist away, but he refused to break his grip.

"Morrin, let your hair down . . . let yourself go for once. What just happened between us was—" He broke off, then said, "It was good. It takes two to start a fire like—"

The phone's sudden ringing made her jump. Gareth frowned, his fingers tightening on her shoulders. "Leave it."

But the phone had saved her, just when she was in danger of slipping once more under his spell. She squirmed out from under his grasp and picked up the receiver, silently uttering a prayer of thanksgiving to whoever was calling. She had to take a deep breath before she could trust her voice to recite the phone number steadily.

"Is Gareth there?" It was a woman's voice; low and husky, not a voice that Morrin knew.

"Yes, he's here." He had walked over to stare down into the fire, and now he turned sharply, frowning at her and shaking his head to indicate that he didn't want to speak to any callers. Morrin held the receiver out. "For you." She pitched her voice so that the woman on the line could hear it.

Gareth glared, then shrugged his shoulders in resignation as he took the receiver from her. After the first, abrupt, "Sinclair here," his voice changed, took on the relaxed, intimate note she had often heard him use to his women callers. "Oh . . . hi, Cass. No, no problem at all, I just got in, so it's lucky you didn't call earlier . . ."

So Camilla was to be replaced by Cass, whoever she was, Morrin thought as she loaded the tray and carried it into the kitchen. Returning for another load she caught snatches of his conversation as she stacked the tray and put the cushion back on the chair, where it belonged.

"When? How bad is it this time? Well, as it so happens I'm fairly free this week," he drawled. "The last chapter of the book's being typed for the publisher, so I should manage tomorrow."

As she carried the tray from the room for a second time he moved to lean one shoulder on the wall as though settling down for a long conversation. "You'll be there too? Yes, it'll be good to spend some time together," he agreed smoothly, and Morrin, brushing past, was aware of his green gaze on her, though she didn't look at him.

In the kitchen she filled the sink with hot soapy water and washed the dishes. After stacking them on the draining board she realised that she was trembling so much that she had to sit down. What on earth had possessed her earlier? Could it have been the brandy and the single glass of wine with her meal? She was shocked by the passion that Gareth had so easily awakened in her. She had never imagined that any man could affect her so strongly. Until that night her feelings for him had been carefully wrapped in tender, romantic dreams that now seemed bland and immature compared to the intensity of the desire she had known when lying in his arms.

She shivered convulsively at the memory, pushing it away. After what had happened she couldn't possibly spend the night in this house, with nobody else there but Gareth. She got up and hurried into the hall. The sitting-room door was shut but she could hear the murmur of his voice and catch the sound of his laughter. Snatching her coat from the cloakroom she ran into the study to retrieve her bag from where it hung by her desk.

She was hurrying on tiptoe across the wide hall like a criminal fleeing from justice when Gareth asked from the door of the sitting-room, "Where d'you think you're going?"

Morrin spun round with a gasp of fright to see him leaning against the door jamb, arms folded.

"I'm . . . I have to go home."

"In this storm?"

"It's calming down n—" she started to say just as a particularly vicious gust of wind slammed against the front of the house.

"Not from where I'm standing. And I told you . . . your little car could easily be blown off the road or hit by a falling tree."

"I'll take that chance." She reached for the door handle, found that the door was locked, and fumbled at the key.

"But I won't." Gareth crossed the hall and put his hand over hers. His touch sent a ripple through her. "The roads are dark and treacherous, and you've been drinking. I'm not going to let you drive home tonight, and that's final. And I'm not going to offer to drive you," he went on as she opened her mouth to speak. "I value my safety even if you don't value yours."

"A taxi . . ."

"Still dangerous, even if there's a driver willing to come all the way out here on a night like this, which I doubt." A trace of amusement gleamed in his eyes and the corner of his mouth twitched. "I've never had this effect on a woman before. Nobody's ever preferred being trapped beneath a falling tree to spending a night with me."

19

"I have no intention of spending the night with you," she flared at him, panic welling up again.

"I don't think you've got much choice," he told her silkily, then the grin that had been struggling to the surface managed to break through. "OK, perhaps I put that crudely. I meant a night under my roof, not necessarily in my bed. Although for a while there I really thought that we—"

"I don't suppose I've got any option . . . about staying, I mean," she interrupted, and turned away.

He helped her to take her coat off, his hands lingering briefly on her shoulders. "You haven't, but don't worry, I won't tell a soul. Your secret will be safe with me. Shall we go back to the sitting-room and have some more brandy?"

"I'd rather just go to b— to my room, if you don't mind. I'm tired." She couldn't go back into that room with him, not with the memory of his kisses tingling wherever they had touched.

"Please yourself. I left a pair of my pyjamas in the room at the back when I was getting changed. They'll be too big for you, but they're better than nothing. Unless, that is, you're one of those women who prefer not to wear anything in bed?"

"Thank you, the pyjamas will be fine." Morrin said, and fled to the stairs.

"By the way . . ." He came to lean on the newel post, her coat still folded in his arms. "That phone call . . . it seems that my grandmother isn't too well, so I'll have to go to Wales tomorrow to see her."

"Your grandmother has a very attractive voice." The words were out before Morrin could stop them. Gareth's eyes blazed with sudden astonishment, then he recovered himself and grinned.

"This is a night of surprises. I've never known you sound bitchy before, my love. That was her god-daughter on the phone."

"I see."

"No you don't," he challenged her. "Why don't you come with me tomorrow and meet the old lady?"

"I can't. There's your book to finish and post off."

"We wouldn't be away for very long. It won't matter if the manuscript's a few days late." He frowned when she shook her head. "Now what's bothering you?"

She hesitated. How could she tell him that after that scene on the rug before the fire she needed a few days away from him in order to get her sense of proportion back? How could she explain that being with him during the journey to Wales and then in his grandmother's house was more than she could handle?

"Oh forget it, it doesn't matter," Gareth said before she could think up a sensible explanation. "It was a stupid idea anyway." He swung away from her and headed towards the kitchen door. "I'll let the dogs out before they settle down for the night." He tossed the words over his shoulder.

In the spare room the gas fire glowed cosily and a pair of light blue pyjamas trimmed with navy had been tossed on to the bed. There was even a toothbrush still in its wrapping, and a small tube of toothpaste, as well as towels and soap. She washed hurriedly in the nearby bathroom, keeping one ear open all the time for his footsteps on the stairs or in the hall outside, then scurried back to her room and undressed. The pyjamas were, of course, far too large for her. She had to roll up the trouser legs and the arms of the jacket before she could move.

Situated as it was at the back of the house, the room had a view – in daylight – over the large garden. As the storm was attacking from the front this room was quieter than the larger spare room, at the front of the house and next to Gareth's bedroom.

Morrin took a hairbrush from her bag, sat down before the dressing-table mirror, and began to brush her hair with long steady strokes. It crackled beneath her fingers, and she worked on it long after it was smooth and shining, lost in her own thoughts, soothed by the rhythmic motion of the brush.

When Gareth said from the doorway, "I was just wondering . . ." she whirled round with a yelp of fright, the brush falling from her fingers.

"I did knock but obviously you didn't hear me. I wondered if by any chance you had decided to sneak out and get yourself killed while I was attending to the dogs."

"I didn't . . . as you can see."

"Mmm." He studied her thoughtfully. Nerve ends tingled all over her body and she was aware of a blush working its way up to her throat and face. "Those pyjamas suit you more than they suit me," he said at last. "I'm making some cocoa. I'll bring a mug up for you if you like."

"I'm fine, thank you."

"If you're sure." He began to close the door, then opened it again to say, "Sleep well. There's a key in the lock, but don't feel that you have to use it. You're quite safe."

Somehow he managed to make it sound like an insult instead of an assurance.

When the door finally closed soundlessly behind him Morrin took a deep, ragged breath, and picked up the hairbrush with trembling fingers. She felt so drained that she scarcely had the energy to climb into bed. She did not turn the key in the lock.

Lying awake in the darkness she listened to the muted roar of the storm and heard Gareth come upstairs, the dogs thumping ahead of him, his voice low and easy as he spoke to them. She closed her eyes and began to count sheep, but as the bedside clock ticked steadily on sleep drew further and further away.

She tossed in the comfortable bed, finally sitting up and turning the pillow over, thumping it viciously into place. Love-making might be a new experience for her, but to Gareth Sinclair it was a way of life and she had been a fool to make such a fuss over what, to him, was nothing more than a few kisses. The women he was used to, women like Camilla and, no doubt, Cass, who had made him laugh on the phone only an hour before, would have enjoyed the episode in the sitting-room that evening then dismissed it from their minds. That was what Gareth expected, and what she herself should have done.

The problem was that Camilla and Cass and Morrin

belonged to different worlds. The other two fitted easily into Gareth's world and Morrin didn't. Perhaps that was why he had kissed her, Morrin thought, turning over in bed for the umpteenth time. Perhaps it amused him to make love to someone who was unsophisticated and naïve.

The idea only made her feel worse about herself. At least he was going away for a few days. She could finish typing his manuscript, send it to the agent, and have time to pull herself together before he came back. Then there would be another book to work on, taking dictation in the mornings, checking it over in the afternoons, when he was usually away from home. That was what she needed now, a few days without his distracting presence, a chance to return to her normal routine.

She was certain of one thing . . . never again would she stay late to finish work. She had tempted Fate, and Fate had well and truly slapped her down.

If you can't stand the heat, get out of the kitchen . . . Recalling the phrase, Morrin smiled wryly in the darkness. She definitely could not stand the heat. The kitchen was not the place for the likes of her.

And yet, she thought as sleep finally relented and returned to claim her, it had been wonderful while it lasted. Something that she would never forget; a glimpse of the unattainable and a memory to hold forever.

Three

M orrin woke to find the room filled with light. Expecting to see her familiar little bedsit she was confused and disorientated for a moment. She half sat up, staring round the sunny room, then fell back on to the pillows as Gareth turned from the window, where he had been opening the curtains.

"Good morning."

"What are you doing here?"

"Protecting your good name." He had shaved and the ends of his dark hair were still wet from his shower. He was wearing a cream shirt with brown slacks and a soft brown cravat tucked into the open shirt collar. "You were sleeping so soundly that I scarcely had the heart to wake you, but I have to leave soon for Wales and I don't know when Mrs P plans to come back. I thought that you might not want her to find you here, in bed. She's fairly used to finding girls in my bed, but not in this one."

"Is that the time? Thank you, I'll get up now."

"Fine," he said, then, "Did you sleep well?"

"Yes, thank you."

"Good. You look as though you had a much more

interesting night than I did," Gareth said, then grinned as his eyes travelled down to her throat.

Following his gaze, Morrin realised for the first time that all the tossing and turning she had endured before falling asleep had loosened the top buttons of his pyjama jacket. She caught the quilt in both fists, pulling it up to her throat.

"Get out of here!"

The grin spread, and his eyes sparked green fire at her embarrassment. "On my way." He nodded towards the bedside table. "I brought some tea. I find that women like little thoughtful touches like morning tea." He began to leave, then turned. "By the way, you look delicious first thing in the morning, especially in someone else's pyjamas. I don't suppose any man's had the chance to tell you that before."

"Thousands!" She tossed the word at him, trying to match his poise. And knew as the door closed on a faint chuckle that she had failed miserably.

She washed and dressed swiftly, not daring to take time to drink the tea in case he came back. Once she was wearing her blue sweater and pleated skirt again she felt a little safer. She brushed out her hair, which had been whipped into a tangle of curls during her restless night, and tied it back with her chiffon scarf then drank the tea, now lukewarm, before carrying the tray downstairs.

A delicious aroma of bacon and coffee wafted through the house. As Morrin went into the kitchen the two dogs greeted her excitedly, then retired to the hearthrug on a sharp order from Gareth.

The kitchen was a large room, complete with brand-new cooker, stone-flagged floor and a huge Welsh dresser bright with patterned crockery. The back door stood open to the soft autumn morning and the garden had a freshly scrubbed air after the previous night's storm. A few wispy clouds were to be seen, high in the blue sky.

"There's been a lot of storm damage," Gareth said from the cooker. "One of the old trees at the bottom of the garden's come down. It's made a bit of a mess of Joe's compost heap."

Joe, the part-time gardener who looked after the garden, was an expert on compost heaps and had lovingly built one up at the end of Gareth's large garden.

The table was already set for breakfast. Gareth dished up bacon and eggs, sat down and picked up a pile of letters. "You don't mind if we go through the post while we eat, do you? I'll have to head for Wales as soon as I can."

It was a relief to have something impersonal to talk about, and it meant that Morrin could slip back into the role of efficient secretary without any further delay. She cleared the table when they'd finished eating and stacked the plates by the sink.

"You don't have to do that," Gareth objected when she turned the tap on. "Mrs P can put them in the dishwasher later."

"I'd rather get them out of the way," she said, then coloured as he caught her meaning and laughed.

"Covering your tracks, are you? Don't want Mrs P

to know that we actually breakfasted together? My dear girl, she's more broad-minded than you are."

Morrin dipped cups into the steaming water, her face bent over the sink. "I don't want her to get the wrong idea."

"You mean that you don't want her to think that you're just another of my floozies, is that it?" Suddenly the amusement was gone; a hard edge had crept into his voice.

"No . . ." she began to protest, then stopped as he swept on.

"Why don't you change the spare room bed while you're at it? Put the sheets into the washing machine before you start work. If we're lucky you might get them dried before Mrs P comes home. I mean it," he insisted when she tried to argue. "See to it, will you? You might not realise it, but I've got my pride as well, you know. I wouldn't want my housekeeper to think that an overnight guest of mine had actually slept in another room."

Morrin felt tears prickle the backs of her eyes. Did he have to keep reminding her of his conquests? She set her jaw and vowed silently to herself that he wasn't going to upset her. A strand of brown hair, curling at the end, fell forward, tickling her face. She tried to push it back with one soapy, wet wrist, and only succeeded in spreading soapsuds across her cheek.

Unexpectedly, Gareth's hand reached out and caught the curl, tucking it back behind her ear. "I'm sorry," he said. "That was unkind."

"I deserved it."

"No you didn't. Morrin, change your mind about coming to Wales with me. You'd enjoy it, and I'd like you to meet my grandmother."

She turned back to the sink and picked up another plate. "I'm your secretary; it's my job to see that your book goes off on time."

When he had gone out, closing the door behind him more sharply than was necessary, she finished washing and drying the dishes, put them away, then changed and remade the bed she had used. She put the bedclothes into the washing machine then went to the study where Gareth, a weekend case by his side, was looking through the pile of papers beside her computer.

"Any questions before I go?"

She sat down at her desk. "I don't think so. I'll see that your manuscript gets posted in good time."

"I'm sure that you will." He picked up his dark blue anorak from the back of a chair. "Perhaps we should have a talk when I get back."

"What about?" Morrin had switched on the computer; now she keyed her password in and waited as it booted up. When Gareth let the silence between them lengthen, she was forced to turn in her swivel chair and look at him. A sudden, unwanted memory of him touching her, kissing her, made her feel weak. "What about?" she repeated.

"We need to clear the air, don't we?"

"I don't think so."

"I think we do. I'll talk to you when I get back from Wales," he said abruptly, and walked out.

She began to type, but when the front door closed her fingers stilled on the keys. She got up and went to the window. Gareth was walking along the flagged path leading to the garage, the anorak slung over one shoulder, his light suitcase swinging by his side. He disappeared round the side of the garage and she stayed where she was until she heard the deep roar of his car engine.

From the study window she couldn't see him leaving, but she waited until she heard the car emerge from the garage, pause at the entrance to the drive, turn into the road, and dwindle into the distance before she went back to her desk. All at once the house seemed lonely, now that he was no longer in it.

By the time Mrs Plover arrived back in the early afternoon, bursting with news about her new grandchild, the bedclothes had been tumble-dried, folded, and put away. After they had shared a pot of tea Morrin returned to the study, followed by the two dogs, who settled on the carpet in a patch of sunshine. Music from the kitchen radio, Mrs Plover's constant companion, drifted to her ears. The house had returned to normal, though Morrin knew that for her it would never be the same again.

She activated the printer and sat back, stretching her arms over her head, as it began to chatter its way through a chapter. Gareth was a talented writer. He had travelled widely and this book, like his two earlier novels, was set abroad, this time in Africa. Morrin had enjoyed every minute of her work on it, even the final editing.

Kate Thorne, Gareth's sister, arrived an hour later,

elegant in a deep brown trouser suit over a pale yellow roll-neck sweater. She shook her head at Morrin's offer of coffee.

"No time, I'm on my way to collect the children from school. I just wanted to have a word with Gareth. Does he know that Gran's not so well?" Kate sat on the broad window sill, her long legs stretched out in front of her, and picked up the little black poodle. "Hello, Polly my love. Yes, Daniel, I can see you, but when are you going to learn that you're too big to sit on my lap!" she scolded the sheepdog, who was trying to scramble on to her knee. "Settle down, now."

"Gareth left for Wales this morning."

"Gone already?" At thirty, two years younger than Gareth and the 'baby' of her family, Kate was an extremely beautiful woman. Sleek, glossy black hair was swept back into a chignon and her eyes were the same clear translucent green as Gareth's, but with a more Eastern slant to the corners. She was married to a banker and lived some ten miles away with her husband and two children. "I thought we could travel there together. Isn't it just like him to forget to get in touch with me. How did he find out about Gran so quickly? If I hadn't telephoned her this morning I wouldn't have known that she was under the weather."

"He got a phone call last night, from someone called Cass. He said that she's your grandmother's god-daughter," Morrin said, and could have bitten her tongue out. If Mrs Plover had been there she would have wanted to know what Morrin was doing at the house in the evening.

Fortunately, Kate didn't notice anything untoward. "Ah." She nodded understandingly. "So that's it. Did he say when he'd be back?" She put the poodle down and got up, wandering about the room, picking up a page of manuscript and reading it with absent-minded interest.

"In a few days."

"Mmm. So perhaps she isn't terribly ill after all. It's difficult to tell with Gran. She's one of those fiercely independent old ladies who refuses to admit to illness, even at her age. But on the other hand she likes to summon us all occasionally and clock us in, just to find out who cares the most. Pots of money, you see. She holds our inheritances over our heads, just as a matter of discipline. It's all so silly," she added with the casual shrug of one who already had more than enough wealth. "Still, we all love her, even Gareth, though they're always quarrelling. Gran doesn't approve of the way he earns his money. She thinks he should be helping Tom in the family business. Doesn't approve of his lifestyle, either." She waved the paper at Morrin. "This looks quite interesting. Do you think my brother's a good writer?"

"I think he's a superb writer."

"You're not just saying that out of loyalty, are you?"

"I read a lot, and I'm not just saying it out of loyalty. One of these days Gareth's going to write an outstanding book."

"Really? It's funny," Kate mused, "writers are a bit

like murderers . . . you know that they exist, but you don't expect to actually have one in your own family. I should really make a point of reading one of his books but it's difficult to find the time with children underfoot. Talking of which . . .' She glanced at her watch and headed for the door.

"I expect Tom and I will have to pop over to see Gran," she said as Morrin and the dogs escorted her to the front door. "She might be really ill this time."

"I don't think Gareth would have rushed off first thing this morning if it hadn't been fairly serious," Morrin offered, and Kate gave a light laugh.

"My dear, Grandmother's illness hasn't really got anything to do with it. It's Cass, her god-daughter. Didn't Gareth tell you about her?" Without waiting for a reply she swept on. "Cass is a schoolteacher, and she's going to marry Gareth."

The bright oblong of sun outside the front door beyond Kate's smooth neat head seemed to shift suddenly, then steady. "I didn't realise that he was engaged," Morrin said carefully.

"He's not, but Cass has adored him since we were all children together. She was the little one that tagged around after us and got in everyone's way, particularly Gareth's. Unfortunately for him, Grandmother and her best friend . . . who just happens to be Cass's grandmother . . . have been planning the match for years. They're just waiting for him to finish sowing his wild oats. In the meantime, Gran likes to send for him now and then so that she can see him and Cass together. She seems to think that in that way they'll manage between them to wear down his resistance."

She stepped outside and glanced up at the sky. "Isn't it a gorgeous day after that terrible storm? Oh, Lord, is that the time already? If I don't fetch the children now their poor teachers will think they've been abandoned. Bye . . ."

Back in the study everything was quiet and peaceful, as though Kate had never dropped her bombshell. The dogs settled down again with grunts of pleasure as the sun warmed them; Mrs Plover brought in some coffee and Morrin worked on until the liquid was almost cold before she realised that it was there.

At the end of the day she switched the computer off, said goodbye to the housekeeper, and drove back to her bedsit without even noticing the rolling hills and gentle green valleys that she loved.

She had planned to listen to a play on the radio that evening, but when it was over she realised that she hadn't heard half of it. She had been sunk in memories – Gareth pacing about the study, running his fingers through his black hair as he dictated to her; Gareth scooping the dogs into his car, or setting off with them for a long walk; Gareth, immaculate and devastatingly handsome in evening dress, leaving for an evening out with one of his many girlfriends . . .

She tuned the radio in to a pop concert, but the bright, catchy music became a background to Gareth's voice as he sprawled in the chair behind his big desk.

"If Elaine calls, tell her I've gone skin-diving in the

Niger or something like that . . . she'll never notice anything odd about it," he had once said, then laughed at Morrin when the rejected Elaine did call, and she had to think up a more believable excuse.

"Why bother?" he demanded when she finally hung up, pink-cheeked and flustered. "It's over and that's that."

He hated women who tried to hang on. As far as he was concerned, relationships were fun . . . and when they stopped being fun, the two people involved should have the sense to walk away from each other without a backward glance. No regrets. And all the time Cass, husky-voiced Cass, had been waiting in the wings. Gareth already knew where his tomorrows lay.

Morrin curled up on her narrow bed and tried to picture her own future. Could she remain with Gareth, working on his novels, answering his phone, dealing with his letters, working close to him? What would happen when the future Mrs Gareth Sinclair swept in from Wales to claim her man and take up residence in the grey stone house?

A job was a job. She was well paid and she loved the work. She might even have been able to put that one indiscreet night behind her completely if Gareth had continued to play the field and move from one lovely woman to another, the dedicated bachelor, a man nobody, particularly Morrin, could expect to tame.

But now that she saw him as a man on the verge of marriage things were different. Gareth Sinclair had put his mark on her as surely as if she had spent the night in his bed. At the mere thought of his touch her body glowed and tingled, her heart flipped, her cool, sensible mind yearned for him. She glanced at her watch and realised that exactly twenty-four hours ago he had been sprawled on the rug at her feet, his shoulder warm against her thigh. She remembered the way he had turned to look up at her, touched her hair, drawn her down into his arms and . . .

She picked up his latest book from a shelf and turned to the photograph at the back. It was a casual shot, a head and shoulders picture of Gareth with Daniel, the sheepdog. In it, Gareth wore the same black polo-necked sweater he had worn the night of the storm, and his hair was tousled, highlighting his rugged good looks. Although the photograph was in black and white his eyes had that clear quality that told of a pure blue or green.

Morrin traced the features on the book jacket with a gentle fingertip, remembering how he had done exactly that to her face in the candlelight. To him, a kiss passed the time and one woman was very like another . . . with the possible exception of Cass. Marooned in the house with Morrin he had amused himself, that was all. It was probably forgotten already, now that he was in Wales with his intimidating grandmother and her god-daughter to occupy his attention.

But it wasn't as easy as that for Morrin. She had never, even at the full stretch of her imagination, believed that one man could bring her such conflict, such misery. Her love for him was no longer something that could be pigeon-holed and made to stay within limits. It overflowed, demanded her continuous attention, and she realised that until the night of the storm she had been fooling herself when she believed that she could continue to look on him as her employer only.

"You've blown it," she told herself aloud, putting the book back. "And you've just lost a good job, my girl."

She worked feverishly all the next day, and by the time she went home she had almost finished the manuscript. One more morning would do it, and in the meantime she had a lot of planning to do.

Sitting cross-legged on her bed, she surveyed her small room. She had enjoyed living there, but she had no real ties. She could walk away from this place without a backward glance. And she had to find the sense and the courage to do the same to Gareth. Faced with having to love him in silence, or never seeing him again, she knew the path she had to take.

"Absence," she told herself firmly, "makes the heart forget. And that's the truth!"

She stayed up late, packing her few belongings, taking down posters from the walls and stripping the room of the personal touches she had painstakingly applied to make it more homely.

On the following morning she reached the house early. Now that she had made her decision she couldn't get away fast enough. She felt as panic-stricken as she had been when Gareth had caught her trying to sneak out into the storm.

This time she couldn't afford to let him catch her. She

had to be away well before there was any chance of his return, for she could no longer be in the same house, the same room as him, and pretend that nothing had changed.

Over lunch she told Mrs Plover that she had to go home for a short while because of her mother's ill health, then, seeing the concerned look on the older woman's face, hated herself for the lie. "She'll be all right, but I need to be there to help nurse her. I'll just finish Mr Sinclair's work, then leave him a note."

"Don't you fret yourself about him, he'll manage without you for a few days," the housekeeper soothed. "You look really upset, love. Best to get home as soon as you can, and put your mind at rest. Your mam'll be right glad to see you, I know."

By early afternoon the manuscript was neatly packed and addressed. Morrin sat before the computer screen for several minutes before laying her fingers on the keys. When the letter was written and printed out, her hands were shaking so badly that she had to lay it on a table in order to read it.

> Gareth, I'm sorry but I have to leave and I will not be returning. Please forget about the salary owing, in lieu of notice. Your book has been completed and posted. Best wishes with it and with your future work. Yours sincerely . . .

She signed it, sealed it into an envelope, wrote his name on the outside, and propped it up on his desk, where he would be sure to see it. He didn't know her parents' address, and anyway, it was highly unlikely that he would want to trace her, so she knew that once she got away from the immediate area she would be free of him.

She hugged the dogs, shooed them out of the study, and closed the door gently. Looking back at the house as she drove away, seeing Mrs Plover waving from the front door with Daniel and Polly prancing about her feet, she found tears filling her eyes, blurring her last sight of the lovely grey stone building.

She blinked hard. She would have to save her tears till later, after she had posted the manuscript, seen her landlady, picked up her cases, and gone back to her parents' home.

Then, and only then, in the room that had been hers all her life until she went north to work for Gareth Sinclair three months earlier, she would have the time, the freedom, and the solitude to cry her heart out.

Four

The late December wind was bitter and as Morrin hurried along the busy London street she was glad of her long black boots and scarlet wool coat.

Passing the front of the theatre she smiled as she glanced up at the billboards advertising the coming show, each proclaiming, 'A Sam Kennedy Production'. She had been Sam Kennedy's personal assistant for a year now, but she still got a thrill out of seeing his name up in huge letters over a theatre.

She was so busy looking that she narrowly avoided falling over a toddler roaming at the length of his reins. Patting the small head and flashing a sympathetic smile at the child's distracted young mother, Morrin went on, ducking round the corner into a quiet, narrow side street with nothing in it but the stage door.

When she reached it, Morrin walked in with the confidence of one who is no stranger to a place. "Hello, George."

The doorman looked up from his newspaper and smiled as she pulled off her scarlet hat and ran her fingers through her hair to fluff it up. "That wind's brought the roses to your cheeks, Miss Grey."

"And to my nose . . . it's freezing!"

"Mr Kennedy's in the auditorium, and it's parky in there today so you'd be best to keep that coat on."

"Thanks, I will." She left him to his paper and his glowing electric fire and pushed through the second door, loosening the black silk scarf, splashed with glowing crimson poppies, from about her throat as she went.

The play was in its final, frantic rehearsal period. The stage was brightly lit and the auditorium in darkness, but she knew just where to find Sam. He was concentrating intently on the actors, but he took time to smile at her as she slipped into the empty seat beside him. His hand reached for hers, fingers interlacing, as he turned back to the stage.

The play was a comedy, and Morrin had no doubt that it was going to be a hit. Sam Kennedy was one of the youngest and most successful theatrical impresarios in Britain, and as far as audiences were concerned he had an uncanny talent for finding the right play and the right actors at the right time. Morrin had grown very fond of him, as a person as well as an employer. Thanks to Sam and the busy, demanding life she led with him, she was beginning to rebuild her life, something that, when she fled from Yorkshire all those months ago, she had not thought possible.

After arriving home she had spent an unhappy few weeks at her parents' house, dreading every phone call and letter, jumping when the doorbell rang, even though she knew that Gareth wouldn't bother to look for her. Why should he, when secretaries were ten a penny?

In those first miserable, empty days she had scanned the society columns in the papers, half dreading the sight of his name linked with that of Cass. 'An engagement has been announced . . .'

Her mother had worried and fussed. "You're so quiet, and you're not eating properly. Are you sure nothing's wrong?"

Morrin had explained away her unexpected arrival home and her announcement that she was not going back to Yorkshire by pretending that she had given in to a sudden bout of homesickness, for she could never have told her kindly, conservative parents the truth. But within a month of moving back in with them she realised that her original intention of finding work in the area was out of the question. She had to get right away from everything and everyone she knew, stand on her own feet, start a completely new life. And thanks to Sam she had succeeded.

Now the pain had all but gone, although occasionally she came across a newspaper photograph of Gareth Sinclair at some function or another, always with a beautiful woman by his side. Each time it happened she experienced an ache around her heart, but soon, she told herself, the sight of him and the thought of him would mean nothing at all to her. Time, as everyone said, was a great healer.

She had allowed herself only one luxury: when the new Gareth Sinclair book, *Charlotte Dreaming*, came into the bookshops she hadn't been able to resist buying it. This was the one he had written just after she left his employment, the one that she had not worked on with him. It was good . . . so good that she had read it several times, carefully avoiding the glossy photograph on the back of the cover each time she picked up her copy. And every time she read it she found something new in it, some hidden facet that had been overlooked before.

She was quite unaware that she had allowed her thoughts to return so completely to her past until a sudden blaze of lights in the auditorium made her blink.

"Well? What d'you think?" Sam wanted to know.

"It's good. It's going to be another success." She couldn't let him know that she hadn't been concentrating on the rehearsal.

"I hope so. And just wait till you hear the great idea I've come up with for the next play!" He stood up, drawing her with him. "Did you have a good week?"

"Lovely." She had been on a short visit to her parents.

"Missed you," he said, then he glanced at his watch. "Give me half an hour to get some things ironed out here, then I'll take you somewhere nice for lunch."

Two hours later he grinned across the restaurant table at her. "I hope you went shopping for your opening night outfit while you were on holiday?"

"I dropped it off at the office earlier. I think you'll like it." On the opening nights of his plays Sam expected Morrin, as his assistant, to accompany him. At first, it had been no more than an enjoyable duty, but as the months passed and the two of them grew closer, it had become a pleasure.

"I'm sure I will." He reached across the white table-cloth again and took both her hands in his. "You're good at picking out exactly the right thing."

Sam liked her to look her best when she was out with him, and under his patient guidance she had become much more sophisticated. Her hair, below shoulder-length with the ends flicked up when she worked for Gareth Sinclair, was now cut short and shaped so that it fitted her head like a silky cap, and she had developed good dress sense. Now she said apprehensively, "It cost an arm and a leg, Sam."

"You put it on your business account, didn't you?"

"Yes, but—"

"That's all right then, it's my arm and leg and I can afford it."

"I just wish you wouldn't insist on spending so much money on me, Sam."

"But I've told you, dressing up for opening nights is part of your job, my darling." The mischievous grin she liked so much flashed over his face. "I'm doing it for me, not for you. If the critics see you looking like a million dollars they'll know that I'm doing well, and that's important."

She laughed, glad to be back in his company. Sam's work was his life, and being with him was stimulating and exciting, like a roller-coaster ride. In his early thirties, with humorous grey eyes and hair the russet shade of autumn leaves, he was always active, always planning ahead to the next meeting, the next show, the next challenge.

Back in the office, situated in a modern block and run by a small staff, Morrin took the new dress from its box and held it up for her employer's inspection. It was made of primrose-coloured lace, full-length and deceptively plain, with narrow shoulder straps. Both bodice and skirt were draped in soft, pointed tiers. As she lifted it from its wrappings the material lay in her hands like a cobweb.

"Hold it up against you. You," said Sam when she did as he said, "are going to be an absolute wow in that dress." Then, his voice suddenly deepening, his eyes becoming serious, "I've missed you a lot over the past week, Morrin. You've become part of my life, d'you realise that?"

Morrin flushed, smiled, and gave her full attention to the business of folding the dress back into the box. She was fond of him and she cherished the good working relationship she and Sam enjoyed, but she was well aware, now, of the dangers of emotional involvement between employer and employee. It would be a long time, if ever, before she could even consider becoming too fond of him or any other man.

"Tell me about your new plans," she suggested, repackaging the dress deftly. The ruse worked; Sam immediately sat up straight in his chair and beamed at her, as excited as a little boy with a new toy.

"I've found my next play and it's going to be a winner. Perhaps the best yet!"

"Oh Sam, that's marvellous!"

"And I think I know the perfect actress for the title role. Her name is Vicki Queen."

Morrin frowned. "I don't think I know of her."

"You will, believe me. She and I were drama students together. I wasn't so hot, which is why I had the sense to change direction during the course and turn to production, but Vicki was a natural. She took all the awards going, and it was my ambition to put her into one of my plays. Then" – the smile disappeared – "she married and gave up the stage, just like that. Went off to live in Spain. The thing is, I heard recently that she and her husband divorced, so Vicki's free to take up her career again. This play would be perfect for her."

"What's it called? When can I read it?"

"It's not exactly a play; at least, not yet," Sam admitted. "But it will be, and it'll be great. And I owe it all to you."

"To me? What did I do?"

"You drew my attention to it. I've seen it on your desk and in your flat, so when I saw it in a bookshop I bought it to find out what fascinated you so much. I couldn't put it down, Morrin, and before I was halfway through it I could just see Vicki in the dramatised version. Ah hah, here we are!"

He had been rummaging about among the papers littering his desk. Now, finding what he was looking for, he held it up, laughing as Morrin stared, dry-mouthed, at the bright jacket. "You look as though you've seen a ghost, darling. Isn't this what you've been reading and re-reading during the past month? *Charlotte Dreaming* by Gareth Sinclair?"

"Y-yes, but . . ." Her voice shook. She swallowed, and tried again. "But that's a novel, Sam, not a play."

He brushed the objection aside. "It can easily be adapted. The dialogue's marvellous, just right for actors, and it could all be done on a single set. The main character, Charlotte . . . it's as if she'd been written specially for Vicki. I've been in touch with her – she's living in Tenerife, of all places. Apparently she got a villa there as part of her divorce settlement."

"Only part of it?"

"Her husband was a millionaire," Sam said, then rushed on, "I sent her a copy of the book, and we're flying out next week, once the new play's been launched, to talk it over with her."

"Sam, this is ridiculous," Morrin said feebly. But there was no stopping him.

"So look out some summer dresses and book two plane seats," he said, then snapped his fingers. "No, hold on a minute . . . why don't we ask this Gareth Sinclair to fly out with us, then he and Vicki can talk the play over face to face."

"You mean that he's already agreed to turn his book into a play for you?"

"Not yet, but I'm sure he will. I only got his home number this morning. Seems he lives in Yorkshire some-where. Here . . ." Sam tore a sheet of paper from a pad and handed it to her. Gareth's phone number, so familiar that she seemed to have said it to callers only the day before, jumped off the page at her. "Call him right now, love, and sweet-talk him into agreeing to fly to Tenerife with us."

"Sam, it won't work."

"Why shouldn't it work?"

"You don't know anything about this man!"

"Do you?"

The question hit her like an unexpected splash of cold water. She stared at him, wondering for a few crazy seconds how he had found out her secret. Then she realised that he had spoken in all innocence. This was the moment to admit that she did know Gareth, to tell Sam why she could not work with him in any capacity. But if she did that – the thoughts raced around her mind as she tried to meet his challenging gaze calmly – Sam would expect her to use her 'influence' with Gareth to persuade him to write the play. Once Sam Kennedy got an idea in his head nothing could stop him.

"No," she said. "Of course I don't know him. How could I?"

"Exactly, so how do you know any more than I do whether he'll refuse or agree? It's a gamble, Morrin, and that's what my work's all about. If you can just get him on our side and persuade him to come to Tenerife with us, I can almost guarantee that Vicki will agree."

"That's another thing . . . if she's as well off as you say, then perhaps she won't want to go back to the stage."

"She needs to do something. I know Vicki, she always had to be active. And now that she's been through a divorce it's even more important for her to pick up her career again."

"Have you spoken to her on the phone?"

"I certainly have."

"But she hasn't come rushing back to London, all excited about doing this so-called play?"

"Don't be so practical, Morrin!"

"That's one of the reasons you hired me, remember? To keep your feet on the ground when you get too carried away. Those were your very words, Sam."

He grinned. "And trust you to remember every one of them. But I have an instinct for these things and it's never wrong. Vicki's been through a traumatic time, she doesn't know what she wants at the moment. She needs company and stimulation at a time like this. Look . . ."

He picked the book up from where it lay on the desk and thrust it under Morrin's nose so that she had no alternative but to stare down at the photograph of Gareth, his hair teased by the wind, his mouth just about to break into a smile, his eyes locked on hers. It was the photograph that always appeared on his book jackets. The familiar pain arrived, stronger than it had been for some time, and Morrin caught her breath as it lanced through her.

"Don't you think he's good looking?" Sam was asking.

"I . . . suppose so."

"I'm sure he could persuade Vicki to consider doing his play."

"Sam," Morrin began patiently, "there is no play."

"Tell you what . . . let's find out about that right now. Phone this Gareth Sinclair . . . strike while the iron's hot."

Morrin felt her world begin to crumble about her. "Sam, this is a scatter-brained idea. Surely you can find another play for Vicki . . . a play that's been written as a play, not a novel."

"What's got into you? Just ring the man now. Please?" Then as she turned to the door, defeated, he said, "Use this phone."

The room was warm, but Morrin felt chilled as she began to dial Gareth's home number, remembering just in time to pretend that she was reading it from the note Sam had given her. Her fingers pushed clumsily at the buttons and her panic mounted as she heard the muted purr of the phone ringing in the study of the big grey stone house overlooking a Yorkshire valley that, even in January, would be green and lush.

Please don't let Gareth himself answer it, she prayed. And realised that it mustn't be Mrs Plover either for she, too, might know Morrin's voice.

When, after only two rings, the receiver was lifted, she was relieved to hear an unknown woman, presumably her replacement as Gareth's secretary, give the number.

"I have a call for . . . for Gareth Sinclair." Each syllable of his name was an effort. Her frantic hope that he wasn't home was dashed when the woman said crisply, "Who is calling, please?"

Morrin knew that she couldn't possibly speak to Gareth. "I have a call from Sam Kennedy in London."

Sam, who had settled himself at his desk and was slitting open an envelope with a paper knife, looked up quickly, shaking his head and motioning her to speak on his behalf, as she often did. At that moment Gareth said cheerfully into her ear, "Sinclair here. Can I help you?"

Morrin's knees began to tremble. She thrust the receiver at Sam, who had no option but to take it, then she scooped up the box containing her lovely new dress and fled from the room.

Sam buzzed for her five minutes later. "Why did you rush off? I thought that at this stage in the negotiations your voice would have more impact on him than mine."

"Sorry, I thought you wanted to speak to him yourself," she lied. "Well . . . did he agree?"

His lower lip eased out, a sure sign that he had not got his way. "He wasn't keen on the idea."

Relief allowed Morrin to feel sorry for Sam in his disappointment. He had failed, but it meant that she was free of Gareth.

"Never mind. You'll find the perfect play for Vicki, wait and see."

He looked at her with a mixture of surprise and exasperation. "But I told you, I've already found the perfect play. You surely don't think I'm going to give up on *Dreaming* as easily as that, do you?"

"But—"

"Morrin, my love, you really don't know what it's all about, do you? I want that play and I'm going to get it.

51

We'll just have to soften Sinclair up, that's all." The light of battle was in his eyes, and as he got to his feet he looked as though he was invincible. Morrin began to realise just why he was so successful in a tough profession. "Go ahead and book those two seats to Tenerife for next week, there's a good girl."

"Is it worth going all that way on a gamble?"

"Of course it is . . . I love gambling. Believe me, if Vicki sets her sights on that part, nobody will deprive her of it. Then, since he refuses to come with us to Tenerife, we'll bring her back here to work on him. I've never met the man who can deny Vicki Queen when she's set her heart on something."

He moved round the desk towards her, his eyes softening, and bent to kiss her gently on the lips. "And I can be every bit as determined as she is when I spot a good thing," he murmured, looking down at her. "So be warned. For now, though, I'll settle for a cup of coffee."

Back at her own desk Morrin stared numbly at the calendar on the opposite wall. She was caught between two determined men; which of them would get his own way? She hoped with all her might that Gareth would emerge as the winner in this battle of wills, and that Sam would be forced to look elsewhere for his next play.

As she dialled the number of the travel agency she felt as though the new life she had carefully built up for herself since her flight from Yorkshire was in danger of being torn down – and by the very man who had held out the promise of safety and a refuge from the misery of her hopeless love for Gareth Sinclair.

Five

The theatre foyer was a rainbow of colour, a pot-pourri of exotic scent, as the audience began to gather for the first night of the new play.

These premières were the spice of life to Sam. He moved through the growing crowd, stopping here and there for a brief word, Morrin by his side. "Keep 'em happy," he murmured in her ear after warmly greeting a critic then easing away. "He never gives my shows good crits, but one day . . . who knows?" Then his hand tightened on her arm and she felt his body tense. "Ah . . . there's the man I'm looking for," he said triumphantly.

"Where?" Wishing that she was taller, she tried in vain to peer through the forest of people surrounding her.

"By the door . . . he's just arrived. Come on." Sam grabbed her hand and almost towed her through the crowd in his eagerness to get to the other side of the foyer. "The fly, my darling, has just wandered into our parlour," he exulted as they went, then, coming to a standstill behind a broad back, "I'm Sam Kennedy, and you must be Gareth Sinclair . . . ?"

Morrin would have pulled back into the throng if

Sam's arm hadn't been round her shoulders. Gareth turned, studying Sam with cool appraisal as they shook hands, then looked fully at Morrin for the first time. His eyes widened, searing her with emerald flame. He opened his mouth but before he could say the damning words she cut in swiftly with, "How do you do? I'm Morrin Grey, Sam's personal assistant."

His eyes darkened to a deep sea-green and after only a second's hesitation he took her hand in his. As their fingers clasped a tremor ran through her body.

"Miss Grey," he said, then, "Haven't we met before?"

"I don't believe so," Morrin said levelly, and his brows tucked together. Every expression, every movement, was so familiar to her. And still, she realised, so dear to her.

"Perhaps I've got a longer memory than you have?" Gareth suggested, his voice silky. Morrin freed her hand as unobtrusively as possible.

"I'm quite sure," she said firmly. She had burned her boats now. She had made it clear to him that they were strangers as far as Sam was concerned. Now she could only hope that he wouldn't let her down.

"Believe me, she would remember. Morrin never forgets anything . . . I don't know what I'd do without her," Sam was saying breezily.

Gareth's gaze moved over Morrin, quickly enough to seem disinterested, but thoroughly enough for her to know that he was taking in everything . . . the subtle make-up, the elegant hairstyle, the expensive gown that left her shoulders bare. She could have sworn that the sweeping glance paused for a fragment of a second when it reached her breasts, nestling demurely in primrose lace. A faint smile tugged at one corner of his mouth and he glanced back at her face before turning to Sam. "I can believe it," he said blandly. "She looks very . . . efficient."

A tall slender young woman with wide blue eyes and a cluster of red-gold curls arrived at that moment, putting one hand, sparkling with rings, on Gareth's arm. Cass, Morrin thought at once, but she was wrong.

"This is Alison Wallace. Alison, meet Sam Kennedy, the man who invited us here. And this is his, er . . ." Gareth let his eyes drift over Morrin again before saying, ". . . his Girl Friday. I'm sorry, I've forgotten your name."

Her face burned, not because of his deliberately off-hand treatment, but because she realised, from the way he had glanced from her to Sam, that he assumed that they were more than employer and employee.

Alison looked at Sam with interest, and immediately began working on him, but he was more interested in talking to Gareth.

"About that book of yours," he began, bringing all his persuasive charm to bear, "Morrin and I are flying out to Tenerife on Tuesday to find out what Vicki thinks of it. And I hope that she'll come back to London with us. If we could all get together then . . ."

Gareth looked genuinely astonished. "You mean you're going to all that trouble over a play that I have no intention of writing?" he asked, and Sam bristled slightly.

"As I told you on the phone, Vicki Queen is a very

talented actress and I think that it would make the perfect vehicle for her. It's too bad that you can't spare the time to fly out with us; it would have been ideal to have an on-the-spot conference."

"As a matter of fact," Gareth said, his smile encompassing Morrin as well as Sam, "my plans have changed since we spoke on the phone. I believe I might be able to get away for a few days after all. Next Tuesday, did you say?"

"Gareth, you can't!" Alison sounded as dismayed as Morrin felt. She clutched at his arm with both hands, her lovely face distorted with anger. "You promised you'd take me skiing next week."

"Umm." His voice was vague, his gaze still fixed on Morrin. She was sure that he could read her thoughts. "It wouldn't take long, darling. I could spend a few days in Tenerife and still be back in time."

"Really?" Sam was radiant. "Forty-eight hours would give you enough time to meet Vicki and have a preliminary discussion about the whole thing. And you could always bring—"

"Business and pleasure never mix," Gareth said decisively, then, pointedly, his gaze flickering back to Morrin, "At least, they never have as far as I'm concerned. Alison won't mind staying behind."

Fury made the girl's lovely face look older. She made it clear after that that she wanted to get Gareth on his own, no doubt to try to talk him out of his shock decision.

"Why didn't you tell me you'd invited that man to the

première?" Morrin wanted to know when she and Sam were alone again.

"I wasn't sure if he'd accept or not. It was another gamble, and besides, if I'd suggested it to you, you'd probably have tried to talk me out of it. But it worked, didn't it? He's interested."

"In turning his novel into a play? You think so?" Morrin asked bitterly. She had no illusions about Gareth's sudden change of mind. He wanted to make her life as difficult as possible.

"You've never fished, have you? The fish sees the bait, he gets curious, he wants to know more. The angler's success lies in good bait, and patience. And I," Sam said gleefully, "have got both."

As the audience began to drift into the theatre for the play Gareth suddenly arrived beside them. "About that flight to Tenerife . . ." He pushed a card into Morrin's hand. "I'll . . . we'll be checking out of this hotel at about twelve thirty tomorrow. Can you get the booking to me before then?"

"Morrin will see to it first thing tomorrow," Sam promised him, and Gareth went off to rejoin his escort.

Morrin had been looking forward to the play, but she couldn't enjoy it. She was uncomfortably aware that Gareth was somewhere in the darkened auditorium, and his shock decision to travel with them to Tenerife had completely unnerved her. He never did anything without a reason; what plan was he hatching now?

Fortunately he and Alison did not attend the after-show party, so Morrin was able to relax and enjoy herself. The play had all the makings of a success, and Sam was on top of the world when he took her home in the early hours of the morning.

"One down and one to go!" he whooped, throwing himself into a big armchair. Sam never had more than one glass of alcohol at a social gathering, but tonight he was drunk with sheer success. He was quite right when he claimed that he didn't need happiness from a bottle.

Morrin smiled absent-mindedly at him and went into her tiny kitchen to make coffee. By the time she carried the tray back to the lounge her mind was made up.

Sam had discarded his jacket and bow tie and was leafing through her collection of CDs. They often visited each other's flats, and he felt quite at home here. He selected a disc he himself had bought for her, a dreamy instrumental piece, and after putting it on he came to sit by her on the sofa.

"Mmm . . ." He stretched an arm along the back of the sofa. "Nice to get away from it all now and then. By the way, did I tell you that you look absolutely stunning?"

"Several times."

"It doesn't hurt to say it again." His fingers brushed her neck and moved on to bury themselves in her hair. He ruffled it and the style that had cost a great deal of money and time to create only a few hours earlier disintegrated, framing her face with silky brown strands. "That's better; I hate to see you looking so formal." He leaned towards her but she stopped him, one hand against his lips.

"Sam, I've been thinking . . ."

"Hmm?" His teeth nibbled gently at her fingers then

he captured her hand in his as she was about to take it away.

"Why don't I stay here in London and let Mr Sinclair have my seat on the plane?"

He stopped teasing her fingers with his teeth and sat upright, staring at her. "That's a lousy idea. What made you come up with it?"

The speech she had rehearsed in the kitchen faded from her head as she looked into his puzzled grey eyes. "Well . . . one of us should be at the office, just in case something goes wrong with this play. It makes sense."

"No it doesn't."

"And what use will I be in Tenerife?"

He took hold of her shoulders, gave her a little shake. "I need you to be there!"

"Your Girl Friday?" she asked sarcastically.

"What's wrong with that? Perhaps Sinclair got it right. After all, I was all alone before you came into my life."

"You had a personal assistant before me."

"And a very capable girl she was, too. But she wasn't you. You're different. Shut up and listen for a moment," he added as she began to argue. "I'm a loner, Morrin." He gathered her into his arms so that her head was against his shoulder. "In the sort of life I lead it's a case of kill or be killed. A real desert island, where the natives can be very unfriendly."

"There aren't natives on a desert island," she interrupted, and felt a laugh rumble through his chest.

"Only because I managed to fight them off. And then

one wonderful day about a year ago, there you were . . .
the perfect Girl Friday, cast ashore from some wreck or
another. You were, weren't you, Morrin?"

It was his turn to cover her mouth with gentle fingers
when she began to protest. "Darling, I've worked with
actors all my life and I know when someone's been
hurt badly."

She squirmed away from him and sat up. "Correction.
I'd burned my fingers through my own stupidity."

"Put it any way you like. You looked ill, you were
jumpy, you flinched every time I even thought of asking
questions about your recent past. So . . . I kept my
mouth shut and let you share my island. And then what
happened?"

"What did happen?"

"I got used to having you around. I began to realise
that I needed you in my work, in my life. And" – his
fingers closed lightly on her bare arm – "in Tenerife with
me, next week."

When she shook her head and began to get up his grip
tightened on her arm, pulling her back down. "One day,"
he told her, "you're going to have to stop running away
from me . . . and from yourself." He leaned forward and
kissed her, his lips warm on hers. "Robinson Crusoe,"
he murmured, "wasn't nearly as fortunate as I am."

"Sam . . ."

"Shhh. Enough talking." He drew her into his arms
and let his mouth drift over her face, outlining her
cheekbones, brushing her nose lightly, claiming her lips
in small, soft kisses. His love-making was so gentle that

Morrin was tempted to give in and lie back in his arms, trusting in him and following wherever he led. Sam was safe, and warm, and comfortable; after her bruising reunion with Gareth she needed security and affection.

Yet even as his arms tightened about her she realised that this was wrong. She couldn't just use him as a haven against the abrasive pain Gareth had reintroduced to her life.

"What's wrong, darling?" he asked when she sat up abruptly. There was disappointment in his voice but he didn't try to take her in his arms again.

"I'm sorry, you're a wonderful man but . . . I just don't want to get involved with anyone; not ye— not just now," she said hastily.

"Morrin, nothing's going to happen between us until you want it to, I promise you. But I hope that one day, you will want it to."

The CD had ended. Morrin got up and crossed to the music centre, grateful for the opportunity to move away from him.

"It's unfair on you . . . you're my best friend as well as my employer, but I'm just not interested in any sort of commitment."

She wouldn't have blamed him if he had stormed at her, slammed his way out of the apartment, but he just shrugged and said, "Okay. It's time I was going, anyway."

At the door he tipped her face up towards his. "I don't want to hear any more nonsense about you staying in London while I'm in Tenerife. Right?"

"Right." That one, she knew, she wouldn't win.

"Kiss me," Sam ordered unexpectedly. She felt herself growing tense, but as she stared up at him he repeated, his voice sharpening, "Kiss me!"

At first his mouth held hers lightly, then almost at once the kiss deepened, his tongue teasing her lips apart, his arms tightening about her. She responded, and when he released her she was aware of a faint sense of loss.

Sam said huskily, "That fire . . . whoever he was . . . must have burned your fingers really badly." His grey eyes probed hers. "Is he likely to come back into your life?"

She longed to tell him the truth, to make it clear to him that he and he alone had the power to see that that did not happen. But it was too late to speak out. Sam trusted her and she had already deceived him with her silence. So she shook her head and said, "No. I wouldn't let that happen . . . not ever."

His eyes cleared and he gave her his youthful grin. "Good. In that case I'll wait. I've got all the time in the world . . . all you're going to need," he said.

When he had gone she took a shower and went to bed, staring at the pattern made on her ceiling by outside lights. Perhaps she wouldn't be able to get a seat for Gareth on the plane. Perhaps Alison would talk him out of going to Tenerife. Slim, leggy Alison would look marvellous on the ski slopes, she thought drowsily. So would Gareth.

As she was drifting into sleep she realised that something had been teasing at the back of her mind ever since

Sam had first kissed her. He was an attractive man, a man she liked very much, but those few moments she had spent in Gareth's arms had made Sam's love-making seem bland. There was none of the passion she had once tasted. A passion that was more of a torment than a pleasure.

A passion that had been re-ignited easily, far more easily than she would have imagined, in that single shocked moment when she came face to face with Gareth in the foyer of the theatre. A passion and a yearning that still craved fulfilment.

A year after she had resolutely decided to put it behind her, it was all starting again.

"A Mr Sinclair phoned," Deborah said as soon as Morrin went into the office on the following morning.

"What did he want?" She was not in the mood for contact with Gareth.

"To know if you'd booked his plane seat."

Morrin's heart sank. So he still intended to go to Tenerife.

"I told him you and Sam always come in late on the morning after a première," Deborah chattered on. "He said that when you did arrive he'd like you to take his airline ticket and all necessary information to his hotel before twelve thirty. He said you'd know where to find him."

"He did, did he?" Sam had another appointment and wouldn't be back until after lunch, so there was no hope of fobbing Gareth off on to him. Morrin toyed with the idea of pretending, until it was too late to do anything about it, that she hadn't been able to get a third seat on the Tenerife flight, then she sighed and reached for the directory. Better get it over with. Besides, if by any remote chance the flight was fully booked she'd like to start enjoying the relief as soon as possible.

There were plenty of seats available. Morrin put the phone down and scowled at it until Deborah said blithely, "I wonder if it's true that your face sticks if the wind changes?"

"Ha ha, very funny. Deborah, would you do something for me?"

"Sure." Deborah was a year younger than Morrin, a bright, bouncy girl who held the post of general secretary, and therefore shared an office with Morrin. The other two members of Sam's staff were based in the outer office.

"Go and collect our flight tickets. And then take one to this hotel." She fished the card Gareth had given her out of her bag and tossed it over to Deborah. "Give it to Gareth Sinclair. Make sure he knows when and where to meet Sam and I on Tuesday morning. OK?"

Deborah was already pulling her coat on. "The man who phoned? The one with the dark velvet voice? I'd be delighted! But he did ask if you'd take the ticket over in person."

"I'm quite sure you can manage admirably," Morrin said crisply. "And I have a lot to do today."

Deborah winked at her. "I'll do my best," she said, and went out.

When she returned two hours later her eyes were glowing. "Wow!" she announced as soon as she appeared in the doorway.

Morrin sighed. "I take it that you got to the hotel in time to meet Mr Sinclair?"

"Meet him? We had coffee together. You might have told me he was an author," Deborah lamented. "I felt like a lemon when I found out. I hadn't read a single one of his books!"

"You can't be expected to read every book that's published."

"That's what he said when I confessed. He was really nice about it. But I'm going to read all of them as soon as I can. He's absolutely . . ." Deborah was lost for words, but not for long. "You don't know what you missed, Morrin . . . morning coffee with a real live author who looks like a film star!" She sighed, lost in rapturous memories. "And he's not even married, did you know that?"

"No, I didn't. So you had a chat about his love life?"

"Not exactly. He just happened to mention that he lived alone, fancy free. He likes it that way."

It had been clear from Alison's presence that he hadn't married Cass after all. Or had he? Had the marriage split up already? Questions danced on the tip of Morrin's tongue but she wouldn't allow herself to ask them.

Deborah smiled to herself over her keyboard for some time, then she said casually, "That Mr Sinclair . . . he seemed quite interested in you."

Morrin felt her face redden. "Me?"

"Mmm. He wanted to know long you'd worked for Mr Kennedy and where you came from . . . things like that."

"I hope you didn't gossip."

"As if I would. And even if I was a gossip I couldn't have told him much, could I? Not when I've only been here for six months."

So Gareth hadn't told Deborah that he'd known Morrin before. She felt a wave of relief, then the tension began to build up again. What was he planning? She thought of phoning him in Yorkshire, giving him some sort of explanation about the way she had suddenly left his employment. Then she decided that he might be waiting, expecting her to call, planning the next step.

Finally she made up her mind that it would be safer to do nothing at all. But with every minute that passed their inevitable meeting at the airport loomed larger in her mind.

Six

On Tuesday Morrin and Sam arrived at the airport early, but Gareth still hadn't arrived when they were called into the departure lounge.

"Perhaps he had trouble getting down from Yorkshire in this bad weather," Sam fretted as he brought a drink for himself and a tomato juice for Morrin to the table where she sat. She herself had begun to hope against hope that Gareth wouldn't arrive in time for the flight, but she couldn't let herself relax until the plane was actually off the ground and she knew for sure that he had been left behind.

"There's nothing we can do about it," she said casually. "If he's too late, then he's too . . ." The final word died on her lips as Sam, looking at the door behind her, broke into a broad grin. Turning, she saw a tall figure in blue denim jacket and trousers striding towards them.

"Weather problems?" Sam wanted to know as Gareth arrived.

"Woman problems." Gareth tossed a travel bag on the floor and sank into a spare seat. "Not that I was in a hurry; I hate waiting around at airports." The words reminded

Morrin vividly of the times when she and Mrs Plover had had to urge him on if he was travelling anywhere. Gareth always waited until the last moment, and he had never to her knowledge missed a plane or a train.

As Sam went to the bar to get a third drink Morrin picked up her bag. "I'll just go and—"

"No you won't," Gareth said pleasantly. "You'll just stay right here, honey-chile, and tell me what the hell you think you're playing at." He smiled at her as though she had just said something amusing.

"We can't talk here. Sam will be back in a moment!" she shot a glance at the bar, terrified in case Sam turned round and saw his assistant arguing with his precious author.

"Good, then he'll be in time to join in the laughter. Uh-oh . . . don't tell me you haven't let him in on your little joke? Your childish pretence that you and I have never met before?"

"Gareth, please don't say anything to him about that."

"So that's it. You're ashamed of me now that you've climbed up the ladder of success."

"Up was the only way to go!" she snapped back through a tight smile. A swift glance at the bar showed that Sam was looking away from them.

Gareth tutted under his breath. "Nasty. And unkind. Being part of the theatrical world has warped your sweet nature, Morrin." He leaned across the table towards her. "Now, about me being your shameful secret . . . it isn't as though anything terrible happened to make you decide to blank out the whole thing. No mad wives in the attic that I can remember. So what can it be?" Then, his eyes widening with feigned astonishment, "It can't be . . . surely it has nothing to do with that night we spent together?"

"We did not spend a night together!"

"Exactly, so why feel ashamed of it? To be honest, I'm a bit disappointed about that," he went on thoughtfully. "Given that you left forever two days later it would have been nice for us both to have had something to remember. Although now that we're flying off to an exotic island together it could still happen. What do you think?"

Sam had picked up the drink and now he was turning from the bar, coming towards them. "Gareth, I'll explain everything to you as soon as I can, I promise you that. In the meantime, please don't say a word to Sam. Please?" She hated having to beg a favour from this man but she had no choice.

He sat back, surveying her through cool, shuttered eyes, then said at last, "Very well, I'll try not to blurt anything out at the wrong moment."

"What do you mean, you'll try?"

His mouth curved in a lazy smile, but his eyes were chips of ice. "I mean that you're just going to have to trust me, aren't you? You've cut your hair."

"What?" Startled by the abrupt change of subject she put a hand to her head.

"It was a lot longer when we were . . . together."

Sam had almost reached them. "It was too long to manage properly," she said briskly, sitting upright and trying to get as far away from Gareth as possible without

69

actually shifting to another seat. His nearness bothered her. His body sent out waves of masculinity that seemed to ripple over her skin.

"I preferred it long," he murmured, then looked up with a bland smile as Sam arrived.

When they boarded the plane Sam led Morrin to the middle seat of a row of three and took the aisle seat beside her. Gareth was seated across the aisle, beside two girls, young and pretty and obviously setting out on holiday together. They gaped when they looked up to see him towering above them.

"It looks as though you're going to be stuck with me for the entire journey," Morrin heard him drawl before he slid into his place beside the delighted girls.

By the time the plane had reached its cruising height, the area where Gareth sat had taken on a party atmosphere. His companions erupted in a crescendo of giggles almost every time he spoke to them, and the people in the seats before and behind him had become involved. Even the flight attendants made a point of lingering in his vicinity whenever they could.

Morrin read, talked to Sam and tried to remain aloof from the merriment across the aisle. Occasionally, when she happened to glance over, she encountered an amused green sidelong look. Once he raised his glass to her in a mocking toast and she felt colour warm her face. She didn't know how she was going to get through the next few days.

When Sam left her side just before the plane began its descent to Tenerife, Gareth immediately excused himself to his besotted companions and moved to sit beside Morrin. "Enjoying the trip?"

She turned a page of her magazine. "Yes, thank you. I don't have to ask you the same question."

"Nice girls. It's their first holiday abroad. They're spending a week in Puerto de la Cruz."

"They certainly seem to have made up for your skiing friend's absence."

"Well, you know what they say." He turned in his seat to study her. "Any port in a storm."

She was wearing a perfectly respectable dark brown velvet skirt and matching jacket over a white vee-necked blouse and yet as his eyes travelled over her she found herself putting down her magazine so that she could pull the jacket shut over her breasts. Annoyed with herself, she moved her hands to her lap.

"I didn't think Alison – that was her name, wasn't it? – would have allowed you to come to Tenerife."

"She didn't have any say in the matter. Besides, I'll be back in time for Austria. And I've promised her a week in Paris over Easter if we miss out on the skiing trip." He slid a sidelong glance at her. "She's well worth waiting for."

I'll just bet she is, Morrin thought savagely. Aloud, she asked, "Gareth, why are you coming to Tenerife? Why did you change your mind?"

His eyebrows rose. The green eyes beneath them were wide, innocent. "Because your . . . your boss" – he deliberately hesitated over the word – "made me a good offer. Because I'm curious to find out if *Charlotte*

Dreaming would really adapt into a play. Because I want to know what happened to make you run away from Yorkshire."

"Not here. Not when Sam might come back at any minute."

"Very well, we'll have plenty of chances to be alone together in Tenerife. For now, you can tell me about Vicki Queen. What's she like as an actress, as a person . . . as a woman?"

"The last two are the same thing, surely."

"Not to a man," Gareth drawled with maddening chauvinism. She opened her mouth to argue hotly as Sam appeared in the aisle. He glanced swiftly at Gareth, who had fastened the seat belt when he sat down, then shrugged, winked at Morrin – a wink that said clearly, 'Humour this man, we want him on our team' – and went to join the two girls Gareth had deserted.

Gareth hadn't turned towards the aisle, though he must have seen Morrin's gaze moving above his head when Sam arrived. Now the seat-belt sign flickered on and the plane's nose began to tilt earthwards. Whether she liked it or not Morrin was stuck with Gareth for the rest of the trip.

"Vicki Queen," he reminded her patiently.

"I've never met her. She and Sam were students together and he says she's extremely talented. She gave up the stage when she married, and now that she's divorced he thinks a new play would kick-start her career. Why don't you ask him that question, since he knows more about her than I do?"

The plane gave a sudden sharp lurch, then recovered itself. "Because Sam may be a businessman but he sees Vicki as a woman rather than an actress, and that clouds his vision."

"I doubt it."

"When he talked to me about her he was definitely a man talking about a woman. I'd say he reckons that she can play any part from Cleopatra to Mary Poppins and back again without having to stop for breath."

"Were you always as cynical as you are now?"

"I don't know – was I, when you knew me?" he challenged, then, when she said nothing, "I'm only cynical where my work is concerned. Otherwise I'm as weak and impressionable as the next man. Do you think I should do what your Sam wants, and write the stage play of my book?"

"He is not my Sam, he is my employer . . . though I don't suppose for a moment that you'll believe that."

The plane lurched again and his shoulder came up hard against hers. As she turned, startled, she realised that his mouth was no more than an inch from hers.

"Dear Morrin," he said gently. "You're quite right . . . I don't believe a word of it." Then, again, "Do you think I should write a stage play for him?"

"I expect you'll do what you think best," she said at last, feebly.

"But I want your opinion, Morrin. You know Sam Kennedy and you know me, probably more than most people do."

"Surely Alison knows you better than I ever could."

"Don't be coy, dear," he reprimanded. "Alison knows what I allow her to know, whereas you've worked with me. You've seen me in all my moods, you were there when things went wrong and when things went right. So answer my question, please."

He was right, she did know him well, and yet, like Alison and, she suspected, everyone else, she had never been allowed to know everything about him.

"Sam knows his job very well, and when he says the book would adapt very well to the stage I believe him."

"That was Morrin the personal assistant talking. What does the real Morrin think?"

"I think you should do what you want. It's your book."

He laughed. "So you're determined to stay on the fence. The thing is, could Vicki Queen play Charlotte? Even more important, could she *be* Charlotte?"

"Gareth, I know nothing about Vicki Queen, and I've only glanced through the book."

Her attempt to snub him failed. "Now that you've done so well for yourself in the theatrical world," he said mildly, "I can appreciate that my type of work is too lowbrow for you."

She looked at him sharply but he gazed back at her with innocent eyes. The plane seemed to lift for a second before slamming back down again, and she gasped and caught at the arms of her seat.

"It's going to be a bumpy landing," Gareth said happily. "Look at the cloud out there."

As they descended through layer upon layer of thick

white cloud the plane seemed to Morrin to be plunging too steeply, bumping and jolting as it went. The other passengers had fallen into a tense silence and Morrin's fingers had begun to ache with the intensity of her grip on the padded arms.

"It's just like a bobsleigh run," she heard Gareth say in her ear, "only we can't see ahead. Once when I was the front man in a bobsleigh team the sleigh was taking the bends like a bird, and—"

Morrin dragged her gaze from the window and tried to fix it on something that wasn't moving about. "Gareth, do you mind?" she said through gritted teeth.

"What's worrying you?" A warm hand covered hers, held it firmly. "Relax, you're with me and I'm not going to let anything bad happen to either of us. It's just a bit of cloud, that's all. Nice white fluffy cloud."

Concrete cloud, Morrin thought. She wanted to jump to her feet and announce at the top of her voice that she had had enough and she was getting off now, thank you. But there was nowhere to go to. Without fully realising what she was doing she turned her hand beneath Gareth's so that her fingers curled round his. Then her free hand inched across her lap towards him and he took hold of it, his grip steadying her and drawing her back from the verge of panic.

"Just close your eyes," she heard him say, and she obeyed, grateful for the strength of his leg against hers, the masculine smell of his body. Turning her face into the angle of his shoulder and his neck she genuinely believed that he was right; he wouldn't let anything happen to her.

When at last the plane levelled and the bumping eased she sat up abruptly, embarrassed and confused, dragging her hands free so that she could smooth her hair. The turmoil the plane had just come through was being mirrored in her own confusion.

Gareth grinned down at her, openly amused by her embarrassment. "That was cosy . . . almost like old times. Feeling better?"

She gave a shaky laugh and began to moisten her dry lips with the tip of her tongue, then stopped as she saw his green eyes following the movement. Gareth, of course, would see it as a sensual act, not one of fear.

"It's at times like these I agree with the ancients who said that man was never meant to leave the ground," she confessed. "Weren't you scared . . . even a little bit?"

One eyebrow rose slightly. "Why should I be afraid? The way I see it, the pilot's as anxious to reach the ground in one piece as I am, and where he goes, I go. Besides" – his gaze travelled over her with open masculine appraisal, lingering at the opening of her blouse – "I was enjoying myself too much to think about danger."

She reddened, and wrenched her head away from him so that she could gaze out of the window, beyond the placid, middle-aged man in the window seat. He didn't change, she thought angrily, staring at an expanse of deep blue water below, creaming into white against the jewelled island spread out as though arranged there for her approval.

A few minutes later she was descending the steps,

blinking in the brilliant sunlight. After the air-conditioned plane Tenerife felt like a warm blanket.

Sam was waiting for her at the bottom of the steps. "You seemed to enjoy the descent."

"Enjoy it? I was terrified."

"Really?" His voice was cool. "You were practically on Sinclair's lap at one point."

"For goodness' sake, Sam, he was only trying to stop me from making a fool of myself. And I didn't ask him to sit beside me, remember."

"I don't know that; I wasn't there."

"Exactly, you weren't there."

"I'm sorry, love." He put an arm about her and hugged her to him. "I'm just feeling a bit edgy now that we're here. If we don't get Vicki and Sinclair to agree over this play I'll have lost a wonderful chance." He dropped a swift kiss on her cheek. "Here we go, my darling . . . and here's to a successful outcome."

They had to wait on the sun-baked tarmac for Gareth. Several passengers had left the plane and gone over to the small open bus waiting to take them to the terminal building before he appeared, lingering to talk to the flight attendant, who dimpled back at him.

"Can't resist the chance to charm women, can he?" Sam murmured.

As he came down the steps Gareth, his jacket slung over one shoulder and his shirt open at the throat, took time to look up at the clear blue sky and across to the low hills behind the buildings. A faint breeze caught at his black hair and ruffled it about his forehead as he loped unhurriedly to where Sam and Morrin were waiting for him.

Standing there, in the circle of Sam's arm, Morrin sensed a pang of real fear. She had built up a good life for herself, a happy life. And she knew, without a doubt, that the man moving down towards her had the ability and, despite his kindness during the plane's bumpy descent, the ruthlessness to destroy everything she had, if he so chose.

Seven

An elderly Spaniard greeted them smilingly in the airport foyer, introducing himself as Jaime and explaining in thickly accented English that he and his wife Maria looked after Vicki Queen's villa.

To Morrin's relief Gareth elected to sit in the front of the car. The drive to the villa took about an hour, and firstly took them through barren landscape seared with angry orange and red rock and soil. Then, after they had driven through the bustling port of Santa Cruz, they reached the lush side of the island. Here, vines, trees and flowers fought to cover every inch of the rich soil. The flowering plants cascaded down walls as white as snow to pour their reds and yellows, pinks and blues, on to the dusty ground. Orange and lemon trees grew in little walled gardens, scarlet Christmas Stars splashed colour across the sunny landscape and proud exotic Bird of Paradise flowers raised their bright orange heads above shorter blossoms.

Soon the banana plantations appeared, with most of the short plants carrying bunches of ripening fruit. It was a paradise overlooked by Teide, the volcano that had shaped this beautiful island. Craning her neck, Morrin glimpsed its snowy peak now and then through the cloudy shawl it wore that day.

Vicki Queen's villa was one of a colony of deceptively plain white houses clustered on a hillside by the sea near Puerto de la Cruz. Each house was surrounded by tall trees, guaranteeing privacy, and across the road the sea pounded and raged on a natural bay guarded by tall cliffs and floored by black silky volcanic sand. The strength of the waves seemed out of place on such a hot, sunny day, but Jaime explained that they were the aftermath of a storm that had hit the island, causing the cloud layer they had flown through.

"There's nothing like a good storm to clear the air, is there?" Gareth said lightly, turning in his seat to beam at Morrin as the car turned into a courtyard where Jaime's wife Maria was waiting at the door to greet them.

The house was square and solid, with brown shutters. The interior was spacious and cool, tiled underfoot and furnished in the beautiful Spanish style, the wood gleaming from years of careful polishing. The walls were bright with paintings and hanging plants and in the lounge, two wide shallow steps down from the hallway, Vicki Queen herself waited to receive them.

There was no other word for it, Morrin decided, as their hostess advanced on Sam, hands outstretched. She wore a scarlet caftan cut low in front to show off her magnificent breasts, and her long black hair hung loose, rippling down her back like a waterfall. Her face and elegant bare feet were coffee coloured and she wore no make-up. She was taller than Morrin, almost Sam's height, and quite flawlessly beautiful.

If Morrin had not already known that the actress was in her late twenties, she would have thought her a good eight years younger. Vicki's small fine hands were scarlet-tipped, and as she put her arms about Sam's neck the wide sleeves of the caftan fell back, exposing rounded tanned forearms.

"Darling . . ." Her voice was husky and rich. "How wonderful to see you again!"

"And you, Vicki." He kissed her on both cheeks then held her back so that he could see her. "How are you, my dear?"

"Divorce," Vicki said sweetly, "becomes me, don't you think?" Then she turned to Gareth, her bright eyes scanning his face. "So . . . this is the clever man who wrote *Charlotte Dreaming*."

How could any man, including Gareth Sinclair, resist this woman, Morrin thought bleakly. If she wanted to play Charlotte she would, and Morrin would have to get used to the idea of seeing a lot more of Gareth . . . unless, once again, she ran away from a job she loved.

She watched as Gareth took Vicki's hands in his, studying her openly. Under his gaze she seemed to grow lovelier and more sensuous, her own eyes roaming boldly over his face, his throat, the smooth chest visible below his partially unbuttoned shirt, then back to his face. It was a meeting between two supremely self-confident people, and Morrin almost felt like an interloper.

Flicking a sidelong glance at Sam she was surprised

to see a mixture of expressions flitting over his face as he watched the two people he had been so anxious to bring together. There was approval at Vicki's obvious interest, and yet there was resentment there as well. Something like the same look he had worn earlier when he waited at the foot of the plane steps for Morrin. She realised with surprise that although he needed Gareth Sinclair, Sam didn't like the man much.

"I approve of him, Sam," Vicki said at just that moment.

Gareth laughed. "Sorry, I'm not for sale, though I'm always interested in considering a good offer," he told her. "But the best offer at the moment would be a shower and a drink, in that order. The small talk can wait."

"Of course, you must all be tired, and hot. And you must be Morrin." Vicki finally noticed her.

"Yes, I am."

"Sam's right hand."

"And a very good right hand, too," Sam put in.

"Good. He needs looking after, don't you, darling?" Vicki released Gareth's hands in order to link arms with Sam, turning him so that the two of them faced Morrin as a unit. "Now . . . you must be anxious to freshen up. Sam, I've put you in the room next to mine, and you're in the guest house, Gareth. We're having dinner tonight in a good restaurant in Puerto. I've booked a table. Come along. Oh, Maria," she added as an afterthought to the maid, still waiting quietly in the background, "perhaps you could show Miss – er – Morrin to her room while I see to the others."

In the small room with its two narrow windows, one looking out to a side pathway bordered with bright flowers, the other overlooking the front courtyard, the road beyond, and the sea on the other side of the road, Morrin dropped her jacket on the bed and tried not to let Vicki's attitude get to her. The actress had made it very clear in those first few moments that Morrin was merely Sam's assistant and nothing more.

Three days at the most, she told herself as she unpacked. Three days, and then Gareth would be off skiing with Alison and she and Sam would be back in London. If all went as Sam hoped, Vicki would probably be with them, but at least, in London, Morrin would not have to spend too much time with the actress.

Although her room was small it was cool and pleasant, and fragrant with the scent of sun-warmed flowers from the garden. She could hear the sea's deep boom as she unpacked. A tray of fruit juice had been placed on the table by the window, and she drank thirstily before stripping her clothes off and stepping under the shower. Exhausted by the journey, the nerve-racking descent through the clouds, and the strain of dealing with Gareth, she stood for some time beneath the cool spray, letting it wash out fatigue and tone up her skin until it tingled.

When she finally emerged, it was to find that the air was so warm that by the time she had towelled and combed her wet hair it was almost dry. She put on a light dressing-gown and, on an impulse, took her copy of *Charlotte Dreaming* from her bag before settling down on the bed. She had read the book so often that she almost knew it by heart, but now that she had met Gareth again she felt the need to look at it once more.

She was fascinated by the fact that it was quite unlike his other three books. For one thing it was set in England, whereas the others had been set abroad. And this one was about a woman . . . a woman with a strong love of honesty and justice, a woman who had been forced to fight hard to preserve these principles in the world she found herself in.

Charlotte, the main character, was striking. In her own way she could be quite ruthless when necessary, yet at the same time she showed compassion towards those who deserved it.

This book wasn't like Gareth at all, Morrin thought for the hundredth time as she leafed through it, reading her favourite sections. To her, it seemed to have been written by someone who totally understood the frustration that a woman like Charlotte would feel when she found herself trying to survive in a world ruled solely by men. Charlotte had been born early in the century, and her life had been nothing like the pampered existence enjoyed by the women in Gareth's world.

Morrin put the book down and stared at the ceiling, trying to understand the man who had written it. There had been no hint, when she worked for Gareth, that this book was brewing in his mind, and yet he must have started it not long after she left Yorkshire. Not long after visiting his grandmother . . . and Cass, Morrin reminded herself. Cass, the schoolteacher who had made up her mind as a child to marry him. Cass was clearly determined and single-minded. Could she be the real Charlotte?

She was still puzzling over the mystery when she fell asleep.

Maria woke Morrin two hours later with tea and an invitation to join the others in the lounge when she was ready. She brushed her hair until it shone and fretted over which dress to wear; then, realising that even if she was clothed in beaten gold she couldn't compete with Vicki Queen, she pulled out a full-skirted, sleeveless dress of cream cotton with a round neck. Cream sandals and a brown chiffon scarf about her throat completed the outfit, and she kept her make-up and perfume light.

She made her entrance nervously and was relieved when she went down the two shallow steps to the lounge to find that Sam, in an off-white suit over a dark shirt, was alone there, a cigarette in his hand as he studied the paintings.

His face lit up when he saw her. "You look marvellous." He kissed her, and she clung to him for a moment. "What would you like to drink?"

She opted for orange juice and he poured it out then led her to a divan. "Now the hard work begins. Since you're the pessimist of our partnership, you'd better give your views first."

"I don't have any, yet."

"You still don't think we've got him, do you?" he pressed, watching her closely. "I'm willing to bet that you're wrong. I'm even prepared to increase my offer to him if necessary."

"Sam, you won't win Gareth Sinclair round with money. He's involved in a family business . . . he's a wealthy man."

"How do you know that?"

She blinked at him, suddenly realising that she had been on the point of giving herself away.

"Well, I – I—"

"Obviously, your assistant makes it her business to know everything about the people you're interested in, Kennedy," Gareth said from the French windows. "Very efficient. Who did you steal her from?"

Sam snatched at the chance to cover up his confusion at being overheard. "Believe it or not, she was out of a job when I found her." He got up as Gareth came into the room. "Can I get you a drink?"

"I can manage, thanks." Gareth went to the cocktail cabinet as though he was the host in his own home. "That's quite surprising," he went on as he mixed himself a drink. "Who on earth let a treasure like that go?" He turned and smiled at Morrin, a smile that said that this time he had saved her, but next time things might be different.

"I don't know. Morrin hates talking about the past."

"Perhaps it's not worth discussing." Gareth had changed into a crisp white shirt with a dark green cravat tucked into the neck. His trousers and velvet jacket were also dark green, and his hair had been brushed.

Moving about the room, drink in hand, he picked up a

book from the table, letting it drop back onto the polished surface after a swift glance.

"That's the copy I sent Vicki of *Charlotte Dreaming*," Sam said. "As she'll tell you herself, she loved it from the first page."

"I'm flattered." Gareth's gaze swung from Sam with startling speed, trapping Morrin before she could look away. "And what did you think of my book, Morrin?" he challenged.

"Now you're talking to a real fan," Sam's voice boomed out, every word clear, every word damning. "Morrin's read it from cover to cover about . . . oh, I don't know how many times. Haven't you, darling?"

"Now that's interesting," Gareth purred. "I didn't think it would be your style, Morrin. I thought you'd—" he had recalled the exact phrase she had used in the plane – "you'd only glanced over the book."

"Oh no." Sam seemed determined to make things worse. "It was Morrin's interest in it that first attracted my attention. She carried it about with her everywhere. She must be one of your greatest fans."

"In that case I would be fascinated to hear just what you thought of the book, Morrin. Please?" Gareth added winningly as she hesitated.

She looked at him, leaning on the back of a tall carved walnut chair, and wanted to throw her glass at him. Criticism had always interested Gareth, but not praise. He squirmed when people gushed about his writing and for that reason he tended to avoid meeting his readers in groups. On the few occasions she had attended a public speaking engagement with him she had seen him hide his true self behind a polite, studious expression. She could see it spreading over his face now, like a mask, only his eyes betraying his wicked delight at having caught her out in a lie.

"I don't think that my opinion could interest you one bit," she said coldly, and he managed to look hurt.

"But you're a reader . . . and readers matter," he protested, his voice warm with fake sincerity. "Where would we authors be without you?"

Sam's hand descended on Morrin's shoulder, his fingers tightening in a gentle reminder that he wanted this man to be charmed. "Go ahead, darling, be honest."

Morrin took a deep breath. There was only one way to give Gareth a taste of his own medicine. "If you really want to know," she said sweetly, "I thought it was wonderful, simply wonderful! I only wish I could write like that! A gift such as yours must be simply – simply . . ."

Gareth's eyes had gone blank with surprise when she first started enthusing, then they widened in sudden swift amusement. The corners of his mouth trembled before he got himself under control.

"Wonderful?" he suggested, and she beamed at him.

"How amazing, that's just what I was going to say!"

"I thought it might be." His voice was bland but his slightly raised eyebrow conceded the game to Morrin. Then his gaze moved beyond her, blazing into an interest that was totally sexual and masculine. Vicki, Morrin realised, had arrived.

She rose, turning, so that they were all on their feet, facing the woman who waited on the top step as though, Morrin thought with a brief stab of resentment, she expected a round of applause. She didn't quite get it, but the air positively crackled as the two men gazed up at her.

Vicki wore black, a plain draped dress that moulded her lush body from shoulders to knees. The neckline plunged almost to her waist and her black hair was plaited and wound round her head, dragged back severely from her oval, full-lipped face. She seemed to flow down the steps, waving away Sam's offer of a drink.

"I'm starving," she said in her husky voice, slipping her arm through Gareth's. "Let's go and have a marvellous dinner and – get to know each other properly."

They swept out without a backward glance, leaving the other two to trail along at their backs.

"Chemistry, or what?" Sam whispered as they followed. Morrin looked at Gareth, tucking Vicki into the car as though she was a piece of precious, fragile porcelain.

"If that's chemistry, beware the fall-out," she murmured, and Sam grinned and ruffled her carefully brushed hair.

Eight

Gareth drove, guiding the car effortlessly over unfamiliar roads while Vicki, beside him, gave directions. The restaurant she had chosen was in the remains of a fortress with the sea crashing against its outer wall.

At Vicki's suggestion they all had Canarias soup, grilled fish and charcoal-grilled meat with green salad. Vicki and Gareth talked throughout the meal, helped along by an occasional comment from Sam. They seemed to Morrin to be having some sort of vocal duel with sexual undertones. They were testing each other, sizing each other up, intent on each other. She concentrated on her plate, feeling completely out of things.

"You've been very quiet, Morrin," Gareth said as they were finishing the meal.

She flushed, suddenly aware that she was the object of three pairs of eyes: one grey and concerned, one dark and disinterested, one green and mocking. "I haven't had anything to say."

"Women always have plenty to say, even when they're not really saying anything."

"Perhaps you've been mixing with the wrong kind of woman," she said tartly. He laughed, and Sam reached out to cover Morrin's hand with his own.

"You'll find that Morrin's more of a thinker. She knows when to keep her own counsel."

"You could be right," Gareth agreed with hidden emphasis that only he and Morrin recognised. Then, "It's Irish, isn't it? Your name."

"I believe so." She was nervous, unsure of his next move.

"Yes, it is. It means 'long-haired'. Only . . ." He reached towards her and his fingers trailed lightly down the length of her hair. The touch was so unexpected that she almost flinched away from it, and so disturbingly sensuous that she wanted to cry out. It set up a hunger that shocked and frightened her, and yet Vicki and Sam did not seem to notice anything.

"Only that isn't really true in your case, is it?" Gareth went on smoothly, seemingly quite unaware of the turmoil he had started within her.

"How on earth did you know the name was Irish?" Sam asked as Morrin fought against a mad desire to catch Gareth's hand and hold it against her cheek.

"I've always been interested in names."

"About *Charlotte Dreaming* . . ." Vicki broke in impatiently, her dark eyes irritated. Vicki Queen liked to be in the spotlight, Morrin realised, whether she was on or off stage.

"What about it?" There was a faint edge to Gareth's voice, a faint darkening of his clear eyes – both signs that he was annoyed.

"Sam was quite right when he said that the part of Charlotte was perfect for me. Perhaps it is time that I resurrected my career." Vicki turned the sentence into an announcement, and Sam's hand, still covering Morrin's, tightened slightly to signal his triumph and relief. Then he removed it and gave the actress his full attention.

"That's wonderful news! So you'll fly back to England with us?"

She shrugged, a beautiful movement that lifted her breasts slightly in their brief covering. "I suppose I must stop being a lotus-eater some time. To be honest, darling, I'm beginning to feel just a little bit bored with this island. And Charlotte is a marvellous part . . . I'll be the envy of London." She touched his arm. "You'll make sure of that, won't you, Sam?"

He took her hand in his and lifted it to his lips. "You have my word," he said. "You know that I always wanted to put you into one of my plays."

"I know that you used to say so," Vicki said huskily, her eyes holding his. To Morrin's surprise she saw colour rise up in Sam's face.

"I meant it. And now that I have a second chance I won't throw it away," he said, as though making a solemn oath. Then, turning to beam at Morrin and Gareth, he added in his usual voice, "Now then. We must give Gareth as much time as he wants in order to get the play just right, and I'll have to see about—"

"Just a minute, Sam." Gareth's voice was quiet but even so it held an undercurrent that stopped Sam in his tracks. "I don't believe that I want this book to be turned into a play after all."

"Don't be silly, darling," Vicki said imperiously, "of course you must write the play for me. It will be wonderful. I will be wonderful in it, and you'll become rich and famous."

It was the wrong attitude to take, Morrin could have told her that. Gareth's eyes were hooded, his face expressionless. "I don't think so, not this particular play. But I'm sure that there are others, Vicki."

"But . . . why not this one?" Sam looked like a child that had just found the toy it had always wanted, then lost it again.

Gareth opened his hands out slightly, turning them palm up. They were large hands, strong and square. "Forgive me, Vicki, but I don't think you're the right person to play Charlotte."

It was said without malice, as a plain statement of fact, but colour immediately flooded the actress's lovely face then ebbed away, leaving it ashen. For a moment Morrin was reminded of the Disney portrayal of the beautiful but wicked stepmother in Snow White.

"Sam?" Vicki's voice was tense and the glance she shot at Sam was furious.

"I don't understand."

"If you had read the book properly, Sam, you would know why I feel the way I do," Gareth said, then to Morrin's horror he turned to her. "According to your employer you've read the book more than once. Give us your interpretation of Charlotte's character."

Once again she was the centre of attention. Vicki's gaze impaled her like a moth pinned into a showcase, Gareth was commanding her to do as he said, and Sam's eyes were openly begging her to be on his side. She cleared her throat.

"I . . . I don't think I'm the right person to ask."

Gareth's lip curled in a sneer. "Probably not, since Sam pays your salary."

"Are you suggesting that I expect Morrin to lie in order to please me, when she thinks otherwise?"

"If she worked for me I would certainly expect complete loyalty from her," Gareth said coolly, and the words stung her like a whip. Then he turned his back on her, addressing himself to Sam. "You have to realise that the Charlotte in my book is a very ordinary woman at heart. She was a fighter . . . she married the man she loved, knowing that in doing so she had chosen a hard path. She struggled every step of the way to help him to become a success and she fought off every setback that threatened him on the way." He paused, and shrugged. "She is a very special and rare type of woman and I just don't see Vicki portraying her as I see her."

"For God's sake, man, I'm an actress!" Vicki snapped at him. "I can be any woman you want me to be!"

"Yes, you're an actress, and a very good one, from what Sam has told me. But Charlotte isn't just a figure on a stage and she never could be."

"You're talking about her as if she's a real person, someone you're in love with," Vicki accused.

"Characters matter to their authors, you know, and

Charlotte certainly matters a lot to me. More than I realised when I first came here." Now it was Gareth's turn to lift the actress's fingers to his lips. "Thank you, Vicki," he said, "for making me realise just how strongly I feel about Charlotte."

"My dear, I'm so glad to know that I was of some use to you after all." Her mouth curved in a smile but her eyes were blazing as she snatched her hand away and stood up abruptly. "I'm tired. It's time we went back to the villa."

They travelled back in silence. Gareth seemed to be a million miles away and Vicki's anger filled the enclosed space. Sam slumped in his seat, deep in thought, while Morrin looked unseeingly out at the night.

As soon as they reached the villa Vicki flounced off to her room without a word. Sam hurried after her while Gareth strode through the house and out through the French windows to the guest house in the garden with only a curt, "Good-night."

Morrin was glad to escape to her own room, but no sooner had she changed into her dressing-gown than Sam tapped at the door.

"She's absolutely furious." He came in without waiting for an invitation, slumping despondently on the bed. "What possessed the man to speak like that in front of her?"

Morrin sat down at the dressing-table and picked up her hairbrush. "I doubt if Gareth Sinclair understands that actresses' egos are delicate."

Sam was too wrapped up in his own problems to

notice the trace of sarcasm in her voice. "He's living in her villa, you'd think he would have more sense than to be so abrupt with his hostess." Then he added wryly, "So now you can go ahead and say it."

"Say what?"

"That you told me it would all end in tears. You warned me and you were right. How did you guess?"

She stared at herself in the mirror, choosing her words carefully. "That's all it was . . . a guess. It seemed to me that a man who had had nothing to do with the stage might not understand how important it is to you and Vicki Queen."

"The thing is, Morrin, I know that *Charlotte Dreaming* would make a great play, and I know that the part would be ideal for Vicki."

"You'll find another play for her."

"Perhaps it will be too late by then. Someone else will have booked her, or she'll have had time to decide to stay in retirement."

"Why is working with Vicki so important to you, Sam? From what I gather she has enough money to live like this for the rest of her life."

"But it would be such a waste! She's a fine actress, but nobody has appreciated that. All she needs is the right part, and I want to be the man to find it for her. We would work so well together, Vicki and I. I was looking forward to it and now . . ."

His voice trailed away, then suddenly he jumped to his feet, filled with purpose. "Dammit, Morrin, I'm not going to let that man just fly off back to Britain tomorrow without giving it one final shot."

"Sam . . ." Her heart sank.

"Put some clothes on, sweetie, we're going to talk to him."

"He'll be asleep . . . and I'm tired!" But even as she protested she knew that it was no use. "Wait outside," she said. "I'll be five minutes."

Gareth, his feet bare, his jacket and tie tossed aside, his shirt unbuttoned, made no secret of his irritation when he saw the two of them outside his door.

"I was just going for a swim." He leaned on the door frame, making it plain that they were not going to be invited inside, and brushed aside Sam's attempt to reopen a discussion about his book. "It was a crazy idea; I told you from the beginning that I couldn't see Charlotte on the stage and I should have stuck to my guns."

"If we could just find some time to talk I'm sure we could work something out."

"If you want to talk then you can join me at the pool in—" – Gareth consulted the watch on his wrist – "three minutes' time."

"I'm not much of a swimmer," Sam admitted.

"That's too bad. Perhaps you could contact the airport first thing tomorrow morning," Gareth suggested to Morrin, "and get me booked on to the first possible plane. I'll get back in good time to keep that appointment in Austria. See you at breakfast."

He closed the door firmly in their faces and they had no option but to start back to the house through the quiet warm night. Then Sam stopped. "Hang on . . . you like swimming, Morrin."

"Me? Not particularly."

"Yes you do. You spend at least one lunchtime every week at a leisure centre, don't you?"

"I just joined to keep Deborah company."

"She says you're a better swimmer than she is. She told me once that you won medals at school."

Morrin started edging towards the villa and the safety of her room. "Sam, no!"

"For me, honey!"

"I'm too tired."

"What could be more relaxing than a late-night dip beneath the stars?"

"I'm going to bed!"

Sam caught at her arm, whirling her round to face him. "Don't you see, Morrin, that this is our last chance? If you can persuade him to give me just one more day . . . just another twenty-four hours . . . Vicki and I will have time to work on him."

"Sam . . . !"

"Do this one thing for me and I will never ask you to do anything again." He pulled her into his arms, dropped a kiss on the end of her nose. "Please?"

Why, she asked herself in her bedroom a few minutes later, did she let Sam charm her into doing what he wanted? But she already knew the answer. He was a talented man, a wonderful boss. He might even become her entire future one day. But despite all that, nobody, especially Morrin, could change Gareth's mind once it was made up. If he intended to leave in the morning that was just what he would do.

The thought made her feel light-headed with relief. Only a few more hours and he would be far away. One quick swim, one token approach about the play just to keep faith with Sam, and then Gareth would be out of her life for good.

She selected a one-piece suit, pulled on a towelling robe over it, and went out to the pool.

Steps led up from the patio to a paved area where the guest house stood. Beyond the small building another short flight of stone steps led to the sun deck and swimming-pool at the end of the garden.

To Morrin's relief the pool was empty and placid, an oblong of glassy aquamarine water taking its colour from the tiles lining it. The rest of the deck was in semi-darkness, lit by the moon and patterned with shadows cast by empty deckchairs and small tables. She paused, the stones cool beneath her bare feet, and took in a deep lungful of clear air. The sky above was studded with stars and music from somewhere in the cluster of villas drifted faintly to her ears. In other circumstances, it would have been a wonderful night to go swimming.

She dipped one foot in the pool, starting ripples that fled silently away from her, distorting the tiles below as they went. The water was warm enough for comfort, cool enough to be refreshing. It really was a magic place, this island. A million miles away from anything she had ever known.

"Romantic, isn't it?" The voice, echoing her own

thoughts but with an ironic note to it, came from just behind her. She spun round, choking back a startled cry, and realised that Gareth had been there all the time, stretched out on a lounger in the soft shadows. He sat up, arms on knees, his eyes gleaming at her and the eerie light from the pool dappling his torso, giving him the look of a warrior encased in a breastplate of finely beaten gold armour.

She swallowed her fright. "That depends on who you're with, surely?"

He swung his feet to the ground, light and shadow playing across the muscles and sinews beneath his smooth skin. "True, but I've always been a great believer in making do with what I've got."

Unbidden and unwanted memories of the house in Yorkshire, the stormy night when he had come home to find her alone, came to her mind and sharpened her voice.

"I remember."

"Do you?" He crossed the stones to stand before her, his hands moving to her shoulders, his thumbs hooking themselves into the neck of her robe and trapping her. He smiled down at her in the soft half-light and said, "I knew you would come to me."

"You really think that I—"

"—would want to come swimming when there was a chance that I might be around? Not really. I should have said that I knew Sam Kennedy would talk you into coming out, in order to persuade me to do his bidding." His hands moved slowly over her shoulders, easing the robe back before them. "I remembered you telling me once that you could swim. And now, here we are. The night is young and we have a lot to talk about. Haven't we, Morrin of the long hair?"

"Let me go, Gareth." She knew that her voice was fluttery, unsure.

He laughed under his breath. "Let you go? When I've just found you? You might disappear again."

"I didn't disappear, I . . . I left your employment."

The robe slipped from her shoulders to fall at her feet. The night air was cool against her skin but his hands, still holding her captive, were warm.

"So you did. You left my employment without a word of warning while I was in Wales." His voice hardened, his hands tensed on her. "Why, Morrin?"

"Because – because—"

"Because of a shared meal, a bottle of wine, a few kisses? You were always naïve but I never thought you stupid. If what happened made you feel uncomfortable then surely you should have talked to me about it, given me the chance to clear the air between us."

"There was nothing to talk about. Our relationship . . . the working relationship we had . . . was spoiled. It was time for me to move on."

"And then a year later, out of the blue, there you are at a première in London, looking all sophisticated and poised. Not at all like the Morrin I knew. Or thought I knew. And there's Sam by your side. Why is it that our working relationship had to be all prim and polite, yet the working relationship between you and your boyfriend can be entirely different?"

His eyes glittered as they moved from hers to her mouth, her throat, lower. She felt her entire body tingle under that gaze. "Sam is not my boyfriend!"

"No? Come off it, love, we've all heard about casting couches. And you're not going to tell me that he looks at you the way he was looking at you that night just because you're an efficient secretary, are you?"

"Gareth, I came here to swim and if you don't let me go at once I'll . . . I'll scream for help!"

"Correction, sweetheart, you were sent here to talk me into agreeing to turn my book into a play. Why is your . . . why is Sam so keen about it?"

"He knows that it would make a very good play, that's all."

"And a very good vehicle for Vicki Queen. He's very eager to get her back to London, isn't he?"

"He thinks highly of her talent."

Standing close to him as she was, she could feel the chuckle building up deep within him. "You're still appealingly naïve despite the smart clothes and the new hairstyle."

"I don't know what you're talking about. Gareth, let go of me," she said again.

"In a minute." He pulled her closer, his lips ruffling her hair as he spoke.

Morrin twisted and squirmed, strongly aware of his hard body against hers. Then, realising that there was no way in which she could release herself, she stopped struggling and stood submissively in his embrace.

"That's much better," he murmured.

"It makes sense, doesn't it, Gareth? Men like to prove that brute strength wins the prize every time."

He drew his breath in sharply and his arms fell to his sides as he stepped away from her.

"But sometimes the prize isn't worth the winning," he said with a bite in his voice. "You're quite safe, Morrin, believe me. You always were as far as I was concerned."

In the light from the pool his face was like granite, his eyes a green blaze that threatened to burn her to a crisp. She wanted to run from him, back to the comfort of her own room, but he blocked her way and nothing would have made her brush past him.

Instead, hot tears rushing to her eyes, she turned from him and fled to her only refuge, the pool.

Nine

The luminous water took Morrin into a cool embrace that swept Gareth's touch from her tingling skin. She was still heading for the tiles below when a noise exploded in her ears, a cluster of silver bubbles rushed past her on their way towards the surface, and his lithe shape skimmed by, just below her.

Morrin surfaced, pushing wet hair back from her face, and struck out for the shallow end, swimming hard, pushing herself through the water. Before she got there a head surfaced by the steps and disappeared again then slipped past her on the way to deeper water.

She stood up and watched as he climbed out of the pool at the other end. Standing on the edge he paused, feet apart, hands resting on his hips, then his arms swung with easy rhythm and he cleaved the water in a perfect dive and surfaced.

Morrin ducked under, skimming over the glass-smooth tiles, and twisted in the water to see him in silhouette above her, a trail of bubbles foaming after him. He was an excellent swimmer. But then, she told herself bitterly, Gareth could do everything perfectly.

She concentrated on her own swimming after that, ignoring and avoiding him. After a few lengths she decided that she had done her duty and earned the right to go back to her room. She was about to stand up in the shallow end when strong hands caught at her ankles, pulling her off her feet.

Crying out with surprise, she felt herself being drawn beneath the surface and into a watery world. Gareth's sinewy limbs twined round hers, his hands sliding up her back and over her helpless body. For a moment she was on the verge of panic . . . then they were on the surface and she was gasping against his shoulder, grateful in her weakness for the arms that supported her.

"You're out of condition." He thumped her on the back with a wet fist.

"You—" Anger almost choked her all over again, and she had to battle against a fit of coughing. "You maniac!" she gasped when she could speak again. "What d'you think you were doing?"

"Sorry, I lost my way in the crowd." He indicated the empty stretch of water behind them. "I didn't realise that I was going to get entangled with you. Lucky I did . . . you might have drowned, do you realise that?"

"You mean that you almost drowned me, you – you moron!"

He tutted softly, pinning her against the side of the pool with his body. "Now you're suffering from shock." His eyes sparkled as he studied her. "You were in no danger and even if you had been I know how to administer the kiss of life. Perhaps . . . just as a safety precaution—"

"Gareth!" She wrenched her head away and his mouth came to rest on her neck, just below her ear. A tremor ran through her body and she tried to break free but his legs still held hers, fusing her hips against his.

"Why do you have to be so unfriendly?" he wondered, his lips tickling her neck. Fire spread from there to her entire body. Then Gareth, with another sudden change of mood, went on, "However, if you insist . . ."

He put his hands to her waist, his fingers spanning her easily, and lifted her to the built-in steps. She clutched at the handrail, leaving the pool as quickly as she could. To her dismay he followed her, water scattering like diamonds from his broad shoulders.

Taking the towel from her hands he began to dry her shoulders. "We haven't had a proper talk yet, and I'm sure that that's what Sam wanted. Why not come to the guest house?" he suggested in her ear. "I'm sure I could rustle up a cup of hot chocolate."

"We have nothing to talk about."

"But you've not persuaded me yet to change my mind about the play."

The night wasn't chilly, but even so Morrin shivered as the towel was eased almost tenderly over her back. Gareth himself wasn't touching her, but every nerve end was aware of him. She wanted to lean against him and feel the warmth of his body against hers, and at the same time she wanted to run from danger.

"How long has it been since we worked together?" he asked. "Eighteen months?"

"Thirteen months and—" She stopped, biting her lip, as he gave a low, triumphant laugh.

"So you haven't forgotten me."

"How could I? I probably hold the record," she countered. "I must be the only woman to walk out on Gareth Sinclair."

"My dear child" – there was genuine amusement in his voice now – "you're certainly not the first to do that, nor the last, I suppose. But I still don't know why you did it. You didn't steal the spoons . . . I counted them at once, of course. You didn't run off with my precious manuscript. No, you were the perfect little secretary to the end . . . you even posted it before you vanished."

"Let's just say that I got tired of Yorkshire." Morrin stepped away from him, picking up her robe and slipping it on, tying the belt tightly. Then she held out one hand for her towel.

Gareth was standing quite still, considering her, his head on one side. After a moment he tossed the towel over to her.

"You're deeper than I thought."

"How's your grandmother?" If she had hoped that the change of subject would throw him she was disappointed.

"As bloody-minded as ever." He reached for his own towel, the aquamarine glow of the pool behind him outlining his athletic body and long legs. "Why are you so keen on pretending to Sam that we never met each other before?"

"Because I don't want him to use me to get what he wants from you."

He gave a disbelieving laugh. "You expect me to swallow that as a good reason?"

"It's true."

"First of all, sweetheart, you walked out on me, God only knows why. Then you get your boyfriend interested in my latest book—"

"I didn't, and he is not my boyfriend!" she flared at him.

"—so that you can drag me back into your life and show me what a sophisticated successful woman you've become."

"What?" It was her turn to laugh with sheer astonishment. "You really think I'd go to all that trouble just to impress you? Seeing you again was the last thing I wanted!"

"But," he forged on, his voice taking on a hard edge, "I'm not impressed, Morrin, I'm not amused and I'm really not interested in you or in your wonderful new life!"

"I didn't tell Sam that I knew you because to be quite honest I hoped he'd drop the whole silly idea of turning *Charlotte Dreaming* into a play. I didn't want you to come to London, I didn't want you here in Tenerife, and I'm glad that you're going back tomorrow . . . you'll never know just how glad!"

Turning to leave, she was suddenly caught, spun round

and pulled into an embrace that pinned her against Gareth, one wrist trapped behind her back. Her only form of defence was to submit as she had done before, but as soon as she let herself go limp, sagging in his embrace, he muttered, "Oh no, Morrin, it won't work a second time . . ." Then his mouth fastened on hers, exploring and demanding.

At first she fought him, despite the fact that his superior strength made her struggles futile. Then all at once her anger changed to something deeper, primitive, enthralling. She became aware of Gareth's wet body, warm and hard against hers, the smell of his skin, his hands urgent on her flesh and his tongue teasing the soft moist lining of her mouth.

She shifted, easing her body to mould it against his. As his grip altered she reached up to run her palms over his shoulders and his broad back, then down the straight strong sweep of his spine beneath its covering of damp cool skin. She wanted to hold this moment in her heart for ever, to memorise the touch, taste and nearness of him while she had the chance.

It was Gareth who ended the embrace, lifting his mouth from hers, easing his hold on her. She clung to him, dazed. They were both breathless, his deep chest rising and falling swiftly against her breasts.

"So . . . you have grown up after all." There was a faint tremor in his voice. For answer she pulled his face down to hers again.

This time their kiss was shared, with equal giving and taking. Morrin felt as she had done when she plunged into the pool, only this time she was submerged in Gareth, linked to him in such intense emotion that it seemed bottomless.

She kissed his chest when he took his mouth from hers, letting her passion-bruised lips soothe themselves in the drops of water still beading his skin.

"Sam's going to be proud of you," he said from above her head.

"Sam?" For one crazy moment she couldn't remember who Sam was. Then, as Gareth released her, pushing her away from him, she came back to her surroundings.

"You were sent out here to sweeten me up." His voice was expressionless. "And you did it well. Very well indeed." He swept his fingers through his hair in a gesture Morrin remembered well. "For a moment there I thought that . . . but not you, Morrin. You're always in control, aren't you?"

"Gareth . . ."

"Time for bed, I think. You've more than earned this week's salary."

"Wait," she said as he turned away from her. "You can't really think that I would . . ."

Then her voice tailed away as she saw the situation through his eyes. Sam's assistant, Sam's bedmate, as he thought, schooled in the art of charming the people Sam wanted charmed.

Tears began to sting her eyes and she had to swallow hard before she could trust herself to speak. "Gareth, I don't suppose you'll believe me but—"

"You're right, I don't believe you, so don't let's waste

110

any more time. Go to bed, Morrin," Gareth said again, and dived into the pool.

Numbly, she caught up her towel, and went down the steps, stopping when she was back in the garden, away from the glow cast by the pool, to knuckle away the tears of humiliation. She had to go back, had to make Gareth see the truth. She would not have him believing lies about her.

But, on the other hand, what was the use? He had already made his mind up about the role she played in Sam's plans. Besides, he was going away. Did it matter any more what he thought?

She looked towards the darkened house just in time to see a brief, tiny pinpoint of light at one of the windows. It vanished, then came again – the glow of a cigarette. Maria and Jaime, she knew, had their own house a hundred yards from the villa and Vicki didn't smoke. But Sam did.

Morrin turned and looked up at the pool area. She and Gareth, locked in each other's arms, would have been silhouetted against the glow from the pool itself, easily seen by someone standing at a window.

Had Sam been spying on them? With a sudden chill she realised that if he had, and if Gareth had seen that giveaway glow from his cigarette, he would naturally have assumed that he was the victim of a plot. Another wrong assumption. She felt as though she was being smothered by them.

In the darkened, silent house a lamp glowed in the hall but there were no lights beneath Sam's door, or

111

Vicki's. In her own room Morrin bathed her swollen mouth, pulled a brush through her tangled hair, and got into bed, trying to convince herself that Gareth's opinion of her didn't matter one bit. He was leaving in the morning, and she would never see him again.

Even so, remembering those moments by the pool, in his arms, she knew that his opinion did matter; it mattered a lot.

She slept restlessly and in the morning she had to put on more make-up than usual in order to hide the faint shadows under her eyes. She was up early, determined to phone the airport first thing and book a seat for Gareth on the first available flight to London. And from there, she supposed, to Austria and Alison. But that was none of her business.

Sam caught up with her as she went into the lounge. "Morning, darling." He dropped a light kiss on her cheek. "Well, how did it go last night?"

"Surely you don't need to ask? After all, you were spying on me, weren't you? You saw it all for yourself."

He looked astonished, then hurt. "I was what?"

"You heard me."

He grabbed Morrin's elbow and hurried her across to the archway that led to the small dining-room. Here, they were well away from the hall. "Not so loud . . . you know how irritable Vicki can be if she's wakened," he cautioned.

"No, I don't . . . but you seem to."

Sam flushed and ran a hand over his neatly combed

hair. "Dammit, Morrin, do you have to take everything so seriously? I just meant that—" Then embarrassment gave way to dawning understanding of her earlier words. "You saw me at the window last night?"

"Yes I did . . . eventually. And you saw me and Gareth, didn't you? You saw him . . . us . . . kissing."

"Well – yes, I did, but I don't actually know what went on, do I? Did you manage to get him to stay on?"

"Is that all you're interested in?"

His brow furrowed. "It's important. You were supposed to be working on him . . . and from what I saw last night, my love, you were doing a very good job."

Morrin had to blink hard to keep tears of rage and shock from her eyes. It was a moment before she could trust her voice.

"Well?" Sam prompted.

"You shouldn't believe everything your eyes tell you, should you?"

"Damn!" He turned away, drumming his fingers on a carved sideboard. "I was so sure that—"

"Perhaps you should have done as I suggested and entrusted the job to Vicki. I'm not a professional temptress, Sam. I didn't quite understand what was expected of me!" She clenched her fists. "I'm here as your assistant, not as . . . as bait. If you want to seduce playwrights you'll have to hire someone else."

"For heaven's sake, you're surely not making all this fuss over one little kiss, are you? Come on, love, I wasn't exactly asking you to make the supreme sacrifice. All I wanted you to do was persuade Sinclair to give us one more day. So you failed . . . and I'm not blaming you."

"Now I'm a failure, is that what you think?" She tried to push past him towards the dining-room but he caught her shoulders, shaking her gently.

"Morrin, Morrin, how do you think I got where I am today? Sometimes people have to be manipulated a little, and it's worth it when I know that I'm right. This play could be great at the box office, and all I need is the time to persuade Vicki and Sinclair. I only asked you to help me a little, that's all."

"I'm sorry if I let you down."

"Don't try sarcasm, it doesn't suit you," Sam said coolly.

"Neither does behaving like a tart just to get you what you want."

"For God's sake, Morrin, you were doing nothing of the sort!"

"It felt like it." Her voice shook.

"Darling, don't be like that. I don't know what you're getting so worked up about." Sam drew her into his arms, holding her close, kissing her hair. "It wasn't your fault. I'm sure that you did your best."

Don't you care? she wanted to ask him. *Didn't you hate to see another man hold me, kiss me, the way Gareth Sinclair kissed me last night?* But he didn't give her the chance.

"I would never expect you to do anything against your own will. It's just that . . . I knew from the first minute you walked into my office, into my life, that you were just what I had been looking for. You and me, Morrin, taking on the world and winning. Each of us playing our part, using our particular skills. Isn't that what it's all about?"

It was a still, warm morning, just right for the sleeveless green sweater and cream-coloured jeans Morrin wore, and yet she felt chilled. This was not the Sam she knew and felt so safe and secure with. This was a stranger, a man willing to make whatever use of her he could in order to achieve his own ends.

"I – I don't know if I can handle this job any longer, Sam." She turned away from him, moving into the dining alcove. "It might be better if I handed in my resignation."

"No!" He tried to draw her to him again but she broke free. "What would I do without you, Morrin?"

"You would find someone else, someone more willing to—"

She stopped short just through the archway, a hand flying, too late, to her mouth.

"Good morning," Gareth said pleasantly, smiling up at her from the breakfast table.

Ten

G areth sat alone at the table, buttering a roll. A half-finished cup of coffee and a neat pile of orange peel showed that he had been there for some time.

Sam pulled himself together while Morrin was still staring with dismay at the evidence that Gareth must have heard a good part, if not all, of their quarrel. "Good morning, Sinclair, did you sleep well?"

"Eventually. It was an . . . interesting night, all in all." Gareth's eyes rested lightly, mockingly, on Morrin's. "I woke early and went down to the village to have a look around." He smiled, seeming quite unaware of any tension between his companions. This morning he wore a striped short-sleeved sweatshirt and white shorts. The sun danced in his hair, which had been left uncombed in a tumble of curls about his face.

Sam pulled a chair out for Morrin, signalling with a faint flicker of an eyebrow as he bent over her that they might as well brazen things out. Maria came with more coffee and a plate of crisp rolls, but Morrin had only taken one sip from her cup before she remembered the phone call she had still to make.

116

She began to get up. "I'd better contact the airport."

"Why should you want to do that?" Gareth asked.

"I have to book your . . ." Her voice faded as she looked into his green eyes.

"Dear me, you must still be asleep," he teased, an indulgent adult being kind to a child. "Haven't you told Sam yet about my change of plan?"

"Change of plan?"

"I've decided to stay on for a couple of days."

"That's great!" Sam's voice cracked with astonished pleasure on the second word.

"Mind you, Kennedy, I'm still not at all sure that this idea of yours will work, but last night Morrin persuaded me against my better judgement to give it a few more days. And I can't go back on my word, can I?" He beamed on them both again then the smile changed to a faint frown. "There's just one problem . . ."

Sam was glowing with pleasure. "Name it and I'll put it right at once," he promised sweepingly.

Gareth stared down at the orange peel on his plate, pushing it round with the tip of one finger. "Morrin pointed out last night that it would be an idea for me to have a shot at roughing out the play and writing some dialogue for Vicki. But I'm used to dictating to a secretary. I would have to find a secretary who understands English and can work fast. And a grasp of scriptwriting would be a big help since I've never done it before. It would surely be impossible to find someone like that on Tenerife at such short notice."

Morrin sat down again, her knees weak as she realised

that he wasn't finished with her after all. Already Sam was saying, "Is that all you need? No problem. Morrin brought her laptop with her, and she knows the book well . . . plus she has a fair bit of experience as far as scripts are concerned. Isn't that right, sweetie?"

"I'm not sure that I'd be of much help." She was clutching at straws, knowing that they were going to be pulled away, leaving her to drown. "I've never worked with a playwright before."

"But surely it's just like taking dictation for a book," Gareth said. "And you know all about that, don't you?" Then as she looked at him sharply he went on, without missing a beat, "Not book dictation, since you've never worked for an author, have you? I meant that you're surely used to taking dictation, and you'll have more experience of scripts than I have. So you'd be a real help to me . . . if you're willing, that is?" He ended on a note of false hope.

Morrin bit her lip. The green gaze holding hers was pointing out quite clearly that if he had wanted to he could have given her away just then. Instead, he had kept her secret . . . but there was a price to pay.

She had no option but to nod and say, "I'll do my best."

"Your best," Gareth said smoothly, "is all I can ask of you." He drained his coffee, put the cup down and rose. "We'll start this afternoon, shall we? I'll leave you both · in peace to enjoy your breakfast."

As soon as Gareth had gone Sam caught Morrin's hand in his and kissed the palm. "Why didn't you tell me you had talked him round, you wonderful little idiot? I knew you wouldn't let me down!"

Morrin took a deep breath. The sooner she told him the truth the better. "Sam, about Gareth. I . . ."

"I know, I know, you don't like him for some reason and you don't like the idea of having to work with him. But just hang on for a couple of days . . . please? For me?" He kissed her hand again, finger by finger. "I am so sorry, my darling; I should have trusted you. Let's have dinner tonight, just the two of us."

"Sam, will you listen to—"

"On the other hand, perhaps we should stay close to Gareth and Vicki for the moment, just to keep them both sweet. I'll take her shopping this afternoon; she loves shops."

Vicki breakfasted in her room and joined her guests on the sun deck shortly before lunch, wearing a skimpy lilac bikini that revealed that she was an even coffee brown all over.

When Sam, who had been waiting impatiently for her, blurted out his news she merely handed him a bottle of lotion and said, "Rub that on my back, will you, darling?" then stretched out on a lounger.

"I thought you'd be thrilled by our news." He lifted her long dark hair from her shoulders and spread it carefully to one side as she settled herself face down. Vicki's hair was like smoke, Morrin thought idly; it seemed to take in the sunlight and hold it captive, but it wasn't as glossy or as soft looking as Gareth's.

119

She and Sam had recently left the pool but Gareth was still in the water, covering length after length with his effortless crawl.

"I thought he would change his mind," Vicki said sleepily, then made a purring noise deep in her throat as Sam's long-fingered hands moved gently over her back. "Mmm, nice. Just a little firmer."

"All we have to do now is to get a workable script, and we're all set."

Vicki said nothing until he had finished working on her back. Then she turned over and sat up, holding her hand out for the bottle.

"We're not quite all set, Sam." She tipped some lotion on to her fingertips and began to cream her arms and shoulders with long caressing strokes.

"No?" He was still kneeling beside her like a slave attending an Egyptian queen. Vicki, with her lush brown body and long black hair, her eyes hidden behind enormous sunglasses and her mouth enigmatic, could have played the part of Cleopatra the Egyptian temptress easily.

"You still have to persuade me," she said now.

Sam's face fell. "But you said last night that you wanted to play Charlotte."

"That was before Gareth" – Vicki turned and looked at the dark head cleaving the water in the pool – "decided that I wasn't good enough to be the damned woman."

"He didn't say that, darling!"

"Are you suggesting that I imagined it?" Vicki's voice

was acidic now, and Sam cast an imploring glance at Morrin.

"I believe that what Gareth meant," she said reluctantly, "was that he wondered if you knew Charlotte's character well enough to tune in to its various facets."

"Exactly!"

"That," Vicki said, "was not what it sounded like to me."

"Sweetheart," Sam coaxed, sounding just as he had earlier, when Morrin had accused him of using her to sweeten Gareth, "the important thing is that he's changed his mind. Now he wants to stay here and do some work on the play."

At that moment Gareth's hands caught the edge of the pool and he lifted himself out effortlessly, water streaming from his hair and face and rippling down his body as he stood up.

Vicki's sunglasses turned in his direction. "I hear that you're going to stay on, after all."

He grinned down at her. "Yes, for a day or two, but I'm not promising you a play, as yet."

She took the glasses off and eyed him from head to foot, then deliberately ran the tip of her tongue over her lower lip before saying in a sultry voice, "And I'm not promising you an actress . . . as yet."

His brows lifted slightly. "So you want us to coax you, is that the idea?"

"That" – Vicki shook a few drops of lotion from the bottle and smoothed it over her throat, then down over the full ripe swell of her breasts – "is the idea."

Her slim manicured hands caressed her body sensuously. Both men watched her, and neither looked up when Morrin rose and walked to the edge of the pool.

"I like to be coaxed," she heard Vicki say, just before she dived into the water.

After lunch, which was served by the pool, Morrin showered and changed into a blouse and light cotton slacks then made for the guest house. She had no option but to work with Gareth, so she might as well get it over with as quickly as possible.

The guest house door was ajar, the room flooded with sunshine. The buzz of an electric razor sounded from the bathroom. That door, too, was open, and Gareth, still in his black bathing trunks, was shaving, his back to her. As the mirror picked up her reflection behind him his eyes flickered briefly in her direction.

"Won't be a moment." His shoulder muscles flowed beneath the skin as he moved and his well-proportioned body balanced easily on the balls of his feet. He carried himself with an easy grace that almost made a mockery of clothes, Morrin thought idly, then gave herself a mental shake and leaned on the door frame, her arms folded.

"Why, Gareth? Why have you decided to stay on?"

"Perhaps I realised that your Sam has a good idea there after all."

"But last night . . ." She wanted to beat at his broad, indifferent back with her fists and at the same time she wanted to touch that velvet skin with the tips of her fingers. She tightened her folded arms as though

122

trying to keep her hands out of the way of tempta-
tion.

"Last night" – Gareth killed the razor's whine, put it
down and reached for a bottle of aftershave – "was really
something, wasn't it? We must do it again some time."

"Last night you had no intention of staying on. Then
this morning you suddenly came up with a ridiculous story about being talked round . . . by me, of all
people. Why?"

"What makes you think that you couldn't talk me
round?" He was still using the same aftershave. Its scent
brought back memories of a life that was over, and a love
that could never have come to anything.

"We both know that I'm the last person you'd listen
to. Why lie to Sam about it?"

"To help you, of course."

"Help me? You could have helped me by just leaving
today, the way you planned."

"You don't understand, do you?" he said kindly. "Last
night I thought that the two of you had cooked up a
scheme between you, then when you had that little
tantrum this morning I realised that you hadn't been
as calculating as I'd thought."

"You were listening to us, to Sam and me."

"I couldn't help but listen, since the two of you were
having a row not two metres away from me." He put the
bottle down on a shelf and swung round to face her. "I
saved your job this morning when you were about to
throw in the towel."

"My job was never in jeopardy."

"No? You seem to have a very casual approach to employment, Morrin. I thought it best," he said silkily, moving into the bedroom as though the doorway was empty, forcing her to skip aside in order to avoid being jammed in the narrow framework with him, "to let Sam think that you had done as he asked you to do. Thus saving you from your own impetuous nature."

"You expect me to believe that you're staying on here for my sake?"

He looked back at her, a half-smile on his face. "You're extremely suspicious for one so young. Whatever happened to your faith in mankind?"

She rammed her hands into the pockets of her slacks, resisting the urge to lash out at him. "Perhaps Yorkshire happened."

Gareth raised a mocking eyebrow. "Are you referring to my lifestyle? You've got to learn to be tolerant, petal. It takes all kinds."

"I had noticed that. Models, hairdressers, designers . . ."

"My life is my own business. It doesn't hurt you or anyone else."

"What about Charlotte? Doesn't it hurt her?"

It was a shot in the dark, but it hit its target. Gareth lost his smile, gaping at her for a moment before pulling himself together. "What do you know about Charlotte?"

"Vicki said last night that she was almost real. She is real, isn't she? She's not just a character in your book."

"How the hell," he asked slowly, "did you work that one out?"

"Because of the way you spoke about her last night.

124

With passion, with . . . with love." The words almost choked her. "Charlotte was – is – someone you know and care for. Or knew, and cared for."

"Well, well, full marks for observation. And now I suppose you expect to be told the full story. Sorry, love . . . we're discussing you, not me. As I said, I saved you just when you were busy talking yourself out of a job. Surely that's worth a little gratitude – to be shown, by the way" – he sat down on the bed and patted the space by his side invitingly – "in any way you choose."

Morrin edged back towards the safety of the door. "Vicki didn't seem to be surprised to hear that you're staying."

"You should have been a detective. You might try it next time you throw yourself out of work."

"When did she try to persuade you?" Morrin probed, though she had already guessed the answer.

Gareth stretched out on the bed, hands behind his head, perfectly relaxed.

"Sam should have stayed at his window for a little longer last night . . . or perhaps not, I'd hate to upset him. Oh yes, I saw him watching us. That's why I kissed you, to give him something to think about. But once you'd left he lost interest and went away. That's when Vicki came tapping at my door. It was fortunate that you didn't take me up on that offer of a cup of hot chocolate, sweetheart." His mouth curved in a wicked smile. "She's not one for messing about, our Vicki. I reckon if she'd found you here with me" – he patted the bed again – "when she came calling she'd have scratched out those big blue eyes of yours."

Morrin felt light-headed. She didn't want to hear any more, and yet she couldn't walk away from him.

"So she—"

"—was very persuasive," Gareth agreed smoothly, stretching his legs across the bed and contemplating his bare toes. "An amazing woman. I tell her that she's too sexy to play my Charlotte and she immediately uses her sexual abilities in an attempt to get me to change my mind. As I said earlier, it was really quite a night."

This was the man she had run from, the man she had spent sleepless nights over, the man whose kisses she had eagerly sought and returned a few hours earlier. She thought of him making love to her and then to Vicki, and realised that neither of them mattered to him.

Morrin's hands came out of her pockets and doubled into fists as she went to stand over him. "And you really wonder why I left your house? How could any woman with an ounce of self-respect work for someone like you? You're self-centred, self-opinionated, vain, pompous, uncar—"

She yelped as fingers clamped over her arm, whisking her through the air and across Gareth's reclining body to land on the bed by his side.

"That" – he was on his knees now, looming over her, his hands pinning hers above her head, his eyes an emerald cauldron of fire just above hers – "is quite enough from you. Now it's my turn."

"Let me go! I'll scream!" she threatened, and he laughed at her.

"You're far too well brought up to embarrass yourself like that. You know something, Morrin? It's time someone taught you that if you can't take it you should stop trying to hand it out."

"I don't know what you're talking about." She gritted the words through set teeth. Changing his grip in order to free one of his hands Gareth began, casually, to unfasten the top button of her blouse.

"Yes you do. You've got a beautiful body, and no doubt Sam's taught you how to use it. But he should also have told you that a woman who likes to tease can get a nasty surprise if she meets up with the wrong man . . . me, for example."

The words stung as hard as though he had hit her with his open hand.

"Don't you dare!"

"It's time you realised that I'll dare whatever and whenever I like," he said. Morrin twisted beneath him, trying unsuccessfully to throw him off, but his weight pinned her down firmly.

"Gareth, please . . ." She began to feel frightened. "You're wrong about – about everything!"

He lifted his head, his eyes probing hers. "You're lying. Again," he said, while his fingers began to work on the second button.

"I'm n-not! I am not lying! Listen to me—"

"No time for that now," Gareth said briskly, suddenly sitting up and swinging his feet to the floor.

"We're supposed to be writing a play . . . remember?"

Morrin couldn't believe it. She lay there, stunned, while he got off the bed and went into the bathroom. He was back almost at once, pulling on a short scarlet robe, looking down on her.

"Come on, then, lazybones. Better fasten yourself up, it's difficult for me to concentrate on work with you sprawled all over my bed and looking so seductive."

Blood rushed to her cheeks as she scrambled up, trying with shaking fingers to fasten her blouse while he watched, his hands fisted on his hips.

"After all, petal," his voice bullied her, "you got what Sam wanted, didn't you? I'm staying. And it's going to cost you."

Eleven

"You're going to have to help me," Gareth said a few minutes later. "I've never written a script before, but you must have some knowledge of how they work."

"I've read one or two and seen plays in rehearsal, but I've never written one."

He shot an irritated look at her. "You'll have to do better than that if you want to get me out of your hair. Forget about being coy, Morrin, I believe Kennedy when he says that you've read my book from cover to cover several times. So talk to me about it!"

"Well . . ." She hesitated, staring down at the laptop's flashing cursor. "It seems to me that you should divide the book up into sections then sort them out in order of priority."

"Sounds like a good idea." He stopped pacing and came to sit opposite, nodding. "I can see that working."

Morrin took a deep breath then said carefully, "Your other problem is whether or not Vicki can play the part of Charlotte in a dramatised version."

"You know perfectly well that I don't see Vicki as Charlotte."

"Why not?"

His eyes probed hers. "You know that already, don't you?" he said, then, as her gaze dropped away from his, "Charlotte is honest and faithful, and when she loves it's for ever. The man who loves her can never care for another woman. Charlotte must be . . . is . . . everything to him."

Morrin's mouth was dry and she had to take her hands quickly from the keyboard and fold them in her lap to hide their trembling. She had never heard Gareth sound so sincere.

"So," he went on, suddenly brisk and matter-of-fact, "Vicki isn't the right person to play her, and if you really have read the book properly you'll agree with me."

"I do," she admitted.

"Then back me up by telling Kennedy what you think."

"I've tried, believe me." Then, as he threw his hands up in despair and got up from the chair to resume his pacing, "But you could look at Charlotte from another angle, taking her strengths and portraying them in a slightly different way through dialogue."

"In other words . . . ?" he prompted.

"In other words, concentrate on the angles that Vicki can develop and let the rest stay in the background."

He came to stand over her, glowering. "Then it wouldn't be my Charlotte."

"No," Morrin agreed, wincing inwardly at that possessive 'my', "but it would be the Charlotte that Sam saw in your book as soon as he read it. I've heard you say before that readers bring their own opinions to bear on every piece of writing, and what Sam sees is a version of Charlotte that Vicki could do. It's quite usual for writers to angle characters in order to make them better stage or screenplay characters and you'll still have the real Charlotte, your Charlotte, in your book. Nobody can spoil that picture of her. And," she added as his eyes glazed over in deep thought, "you would reach another type of audience with the play."

He squatted down by her chair, grinning. "In other words, my love, you think that I should cheat."

"If you want to put it like that, yes. Why not?"

"You clever little thing." Before she could stop him he cupped her face in his hands and kissed her soundly on the lips. Then he got to his feet and began to pace again, this time with the sense of purpose she remembered from the time she had worked for him. "Right," he said with renewed enthusiasm. "Let's start on this play!"

A few hours later they had roughed out the first act and completed five pages of script. It was a joint effort and the two of them had argued, laughed, and fretted together, becoming completely involved in the project.

When the completed pages were printed out Gareth pulled a chair close to Morrin's and said, to her alarm, "Let's try reading it aloud."

He read well but Morrin felt self-conscious and shaky at first. Then as they moved on to the second page Charlotte's character began to catch her interest and she read with mounting enthusiasm, finding herself disappointed when the five pages were finished.

"What do you think?"

"I think it's good. You've brought Charlotte to life."

"We did it," Gareth corrected her. "You read very well. It was almost as if you know her. Morrin . . . why did you run away like that?"

"I've told you, because . . ." Her voice failed her. They had been sitting close together in order to share the pages of script; how close, she had not realised until she looked up to see his eyes only inches from her own.

"Just because I touched you, like this . . ." He held the script in one hand, and now he lifted the other to cup her cheek. "And kissed you, like this?"

Before she could move, his lips were covering hers, holding them in a soft, light caress. She would have pulled back, but his hand was on the nape of her neck, holding her still.

"Gareth," she said faintly when he took his mouth from hers, "this isn't fair."

"But it's very pleasant, isn't it? Tell me to stop, and I will. Promise." Amusement danced in his eyes and she felt the warmth of his soft laugh on her cheek. She felt her treacherous lips part eagerly as he leaned towards her again, knew that her own hands were creeping up to touch and hold him . . . then as a step was heard on the path outside they pulled away from each other so sharply that the papers Gareth held went flying.

"Damn," Morrin heard him say as they both dropped to the floor to retrieve the script. The door opened, and the gust of warm, flower-fragrant air it let in sent the pages eddying about the floor.

"Have you two been working all this time?" Sam wanted to know, sweeping into the room. "Dinner's almost on the table."

"Already?" Morrin stared up at him in disbelief.

"What do you mean already? We've been waiting for you for ages, but Vicki sent me to say that she won't wait any longer." Sam bent to pick up a page that had skittered across the tiled floor to his feet. "You've started, then? Can I read it?"

"Of course." Gareth tapped the retrieved pages on the table to bring them into order, then handed them over, while Morrin glanced down at her slacks and blouse.

"I'll have to change."

"No need, you look fine as you are," Sam assured her, then, eyeing Gareth's red dressing-gown and bare legs disapprovingly, "You could dress up a bit, though, Sinclair."

"Have a gin and tonic ready in two minutes," Gareth told him, and shooed the two of them out.

By the time they sat down at the table Sam had scanned the few pages of script. He was so enthusiastic that Vicki began to look irritated.

"It's only a rough idea," she said sharply. "Not a finished play."

"It's got a lot of promise. We'll read it out loud

133

after dinner . . . I'll take the part of Charlotte's future husband."

Because Gareth stared at the floor throughout the brief reading Morrin was unable to tell what he thought of Vicki's interpretation of the role. The actress attacked the part hard, putting far more into the reading than Morrin had. Afterwards, she found fault with several small points, but even she could not entirely fault the play.

"You want us to go on with it, then?" Gareth wanted to know.

"I would have to read more before I could make a decision," Vicki told him, and he shrugged.

"I can spare another couple of days, but no more than that."

"You have a natural talent for dialogue," Sam said. "It shone through the book, and I like the angle you've taken with the play."

"Morrin has to take some of the credit. I've enjoyed working with her ag—" Gareth stopped short then went on easily, "—against my own instincts, I have to admit."

"Why should you feel uncomfortable about working with her?" Sam asked almost belligerently.

"I knew from what she said earlier that Morrin didn't care for the book, so naturally I thought that her . . . personal feelings," Gareth said casually, "would get in the way."

"Morrin's too professional to allow personal beliefs to cloud her work."

"I realised that, this afternoon," Gareth agreed. Seeing the flicker of annoyance that had passed over his face Morrin knew that his earlier slip of the tongue, when he had almost said that he had enjoyed working with her again, had been accidental. But now that danger had been averted he was teasing her again, giving everything he said a hidden meaning that only he and she recognised. "In fact," he went on easily, "there were times when I could almost have sworn that she liked the book after all."

"As Sam says, I like to do my best, regardless of my own personal feelings." Morrin stood up, anxious to bring the discussion to a close. "I think I'll go for a walk before bed."

"Why not try a swim?" Gareth suggested, stretching his arms above his head. From within their shelter, unseen by the others, his green eyes challenged her. "That's what I'm going to do."

"Tonight I would rather walk."

"I'll swim with you," Vicki chimed in. "It will give us a chance to discuss Charlotte's character more fully. Sam, you can go walking with Morrin."

Gareth shrugged and got to his feet. "See you at the pool later, then," he said, adding ominously, "And tomorrow you and I will pick up where we left off this afternoon, Morrin."

"So how was it?" Sam wanted to know as he and Morrin wandered down the dusty road.

"Tiring." It had also been exciting and exhilarating,

but she could not tell Sam that. She had always enjoyed working for Gareth; during the planning and writing of his books he became totally committed, and although the work was arduous, each day had been an adventure. In the evenings, alone in her small bedsit while her employer was out with his current girlfriend, she had found herself longing for the next day.

"I can imagine. He shouldn't have worked you so hard," Sam said, and then, his voice exultant, "but it paid off, didn't it? He's made a good start and Vicki's impressed."

"Is she?"

"I can tell. She still wants to be coaxed, though. That's why she wanted us out of the way tonight."

"I think I'll turn back now, Sam. I'm more tired than I thought."

"Of course. It's a shame that you're having to work in such a lovely place," Sam said as they retraced their steps. "There were so many places I wanted to show you."

"You still could, if we found a secretary for Gareth. I'd far rather be with you than with him."

"We might be able to do that," Sam said thoughtfully, and her heart leapt, only to fall again as he went on, "but on the other hand, love, it might be a better idea for you to go on working with him. You can keep his nose to the grindstone and he seems to be happy enough with you."

"And what if I'm not happy with him?"

"He's not tried anything on, has he?" Sam asked suspiciously.

"Of course not, Vicki's much more his type than I am. I just don't care for him, that's all."

They had almost reached the villa. He put a hand on her arm, turning her to face him. "Just two more days, darling. Just enough time to establish the play and persuade Vicki, then you'll be free, I promise. This will be the last time I ask you to—"

"Stop saying that, Sam!"

"I'll tell you what . . . to make up for you having to slave over a hot laptop for the next two days, how about us having the holiday of a lifetime later? Wherever you want to go, all expenses paid."

"You mean . . . us together?"

"Why not?" He bent to kiss her gently, the way Gareth had kissed her earlier. Yet it wasn't the same. "Separate rooms if you insist . . . separate hotels if it makes you feel happier. But let's spend some time alone together, getting to know each other properly. Where do you want to go?"

Still half convinced that he was teasing, Morrin snatched names out of the air. "The Seychelles . . . Malta . . . China . . ."

"Australia, Singapore, Tasmania. You choose, and as soon as this deal's wrapped up we'll go. That's a promise. No shop talk, nobody else, just you and me."

"I couldn't," she said nervously, and he kissed her again.

"You could. And I can't think of anyone I'd rather share an exotic beach with. Robinson Crusoe, remember?"

As he grinned down at her Morrin felt a warm glow ease the hurt he had caused her earlier, and as they went into the house together she wished that Vicki and Gareth were both a thousand miles away.

"Go and put on something warm," Gareth told Morrin the next morning after Vicki and Sam had departed for Santa Cruz. "And ask Maria if she can lend you a pair of wellington boots or something like that. I'm taking you to visit Teide and believe it or not, there's snow on the top of that mountain. I've hired a car; meet you out front in ten minutes."

"But we're supposed to be getting on with the play."

"All visitors have to pay their respects to the volcano when they arrive on Tenerife. In any case, I have some thinking to do before I get back to the script. Don't you remember the way it used to be with my books?"

She remembered. He used to toss a bag of golf clubs into the boot of his car and drive off, or walk for miles with the dogs. Or phone one of his girlfriends and arrange to take her out for the day. "You didn't expect me to go with you in those days."

"Today I do. Sam has loaned you to me – and you're going," Gareth said, "if I have to carry you up the damned mountain over my shoulder. Nine minutes."

"You don't need me if you're thinking, do you?"

"I might want to talk to someone about it and you're all I've got." He clapped his hands at her as though guiding an errant hen into its litter house.

138

"Eight minutes. Go on, I'm not going to wait all day for you."

She went, reminding herself as she dressed in a checked shirt and black slacks that it was her job to do as Sam wished. And if she endured for long enough, she would eventually regain her freedom.

Gareth was leaning against a blue open-topped car when she left the house. "Not bad . . . just under fifteen minutes." He scooped her into the passenger seat with none of the gallantry he had shown towards Vicki on their first evening.

They drove in silence for some time. As the car began to climb, leaving the flat coastal area behind, he said easily, "Sure you're comfortable?"

"Perfectly, thank you."

"Then don't you think you should stop sulking?"

"Why should I be sulking?"

She caught the green glint of an amused sidelong glance. "I don't know, but if you get any nearer to that door you'll be on the other side of it. You don't have to huddle as far away from me as possible, you know. We're only out for a drive, nothing more than that. I can't seduce you while I'm driving, and I'm long past the stage of a quick grope in a small car, thank God."

They climbed through pine forests, passing a lorry parked by the roadside. The men working about it were shovelling masses of soft thick brown material from piles by the verge.

"Pine needles from the floor of the forest," Gareth

told her. "They use it for animal bedding, then manure. They're very thrifty people."

"How do you know that?"

"I've been here before, several times. My parents brought us to Tenerife on a number of holidays."

When they stopped at a small tavern for a glass of wine, Morrin, remembering that she was supposed to be working on Sam's behalf, tried to start a discussion about the play, but Gareth brushed her aside with an impatient, "Don't spoil the day by talking shop." Then, when their glasses were empty and they rose to go, he said, "Come and see this."

She followed him on to the terrace and up a flight of steps to the flat roof. From there they overlooked a huge valley where, far below, a large concrete water holder and a scatter of white houses looked like toys dropped by a bored child over the green carpet of the banana plantations.

"That," Gareth indicated a sandy area, flanked by wooden benches, by the side of the house, "is a wrestling ring. The Cuanches, the former inhabitants of these islands, were great wrestlers and the local men keep the custom alive. I've been to a few matches, and they were great."

"There's a mist coming." Morrin moved to the parapet. The sky had taken on a pearly oyster colour while they were drinking their wine and the mist, coming inland from the sea, was a wall of pale grey edging towards them.

"We'll be going above it." Gareth, who had joined

her, turned to lean back on the parapet, looking down at her. "You puzzle me, Morrin of the long hair. You run from my employment just because we enjoyed a . . . social interlude one evening when we were thrown by circumstances into each other's arms, but you're quite happy to work for Sam Kennedy when you're besotted by him. What's the difference between him and me?"

"You seriously think that we're . . . that Sam and I . . ." Morrin stopped, tongue-tied.

"You have such an easy way with words," Gareth said smoothly. "If you're trying to tell me that the two of you are lovers, I already know it and I'm not in the least bit shocked. Long live the permissive society, I say."

"Only because it suits you very well." It was difficult to have a logical conversation with this man. She leaned her elbows on the parapet and gazed down at the valley, refusing to look at him. The mist was rolling towards them steadily now, covering houses and banana plantations as it advanced. "Sam is my boss, and nothing more. Do you understand?"

"I do, but I don't think Vicki does." Gareth said. "Haven't you noticed the way she looks at you sometimes, as if she wouldn't mind pushing you into the pool and holding you under? I'd watch my step if I was you."

"Vicki Queen has no time for other women."

"No time for you, certainly. Perhaps it's as well that I'm staying on to mind your back, since you seem to be oblivious to what's going on around you."

The mist seemed to jump the final fifty yards.

Suddenly it was all around them, reaching out with chilly fingers to touch Morrin's face. She couldn't see anything beyond the wall. It was as though the two of them were alone in the world. She shivered at the thought.

"Cold?" Gareth reached out as though to enfold her in the warmth of his arms but she pulled away.

"You stayed for one reason and one reason only."

The sudden dampness had silvered his hair. "I did? Do tell."

"Because you knew that it was the last thing I wanted."

"Clever," said Gareth. Then, putting a hand beneath her arm, "We'd best be on our way to pay our respects to Teide."

Twelve

O nce back at the car Morrin was glad to pull on her blue sweater and white cagoule, tucking her damp hair inside the hood. Gareth put on a crimson sweater but left his anorak on the back seat.

A few miles onward and upward they broke through the damp clinging mist into an unexpectedly clear cold world with the sun shining from a blue sky. At this height they were in line with the tops of the giant firs from the valley below, and cloud lapped the crowns of the trees like a sea breaking on the shore. Above them, Teide's magnificent snow-capped peak dominated everything.

They drove through a lunar landscape of volcanic rock in every shade of brown, fawn and black before leaving the car and taking a cable-car ride to the top of the mountain.

"It's hard to believe that people are sunbathing down there." Gareth nodded at the layer of cloud below as they crunched through crisp dazzling snow. He suddenly veered to one side and began to climb one of the strangely shaped fingers of rock formed by the volcanic eruption, balancing himself easily on the very top, his dark head outlined by the vivid blue of the sky.

"It's almost like being in Austria," he called down to her.

"With the wrong company."

"You'll do to be getting on with," he said casually, then, when he had rejoined her, "Can you ski?"

"I've never tried."

"I could teach you. You'd enjoy it. The snow and the sun, the relaxing, lazy evenings and a soft warm bed at the end of the day . . ." His voice deepened, and when she looked up at him she saw that his eyes had darkened. "Oh, I could teach you such a lot . . ."

"And what about Alison?"

He laughed. "Alison was not part of the picture I was painting. You're always so practical, aren't you? Do you never fantasise, Morrin?"

"Often," she retorted, and he caught her fingers in his, pulling her on through the snow with him.

"About Sam?"

"Sam is *not*—"

"Say that often enough and I might begin to believe you," Gareth said. "Or perhaps not." She found herself swung round to stand before him so that they were face to face. "Morrin, he's a lot older than you are."

"Sam Kennedy is thirty-one and you are—"

"I can't deny that I've had my thirty-second birthday since we . . . parted company," he admitted. "I was looking for a card but you didn't send one."

"Maybe I did, and it got lost in the crowd."

"I would have noticed." He gave her hands, still in his, a little shake. "Anyway, it's not my advancing years we're discussing, it's Sam Kennedy. The theatrical world is different from anything you've been used to before, Morrin. These people live in a romantic world of make-believe. They fall in and out of love very easily."

"You're trying to tell me that Sam's shallow and he'll break my heart because I'm too naïve for my own good?"

"I didn't say he's shallow, I just meant that he's more . . . experienced in his particular world than you are. Despite what you believe, Morrin Grey, I like you and I don't want to see you getting hurt."

"You won't." She broke free of him and strode on over the dazzling snow, glad of the boots Maria had found for her.

"Why does it have to be one rule for you and another for me?" she wanted to know when he caught up with her.

"Because you're too young to know what it's all about."

Exasperated beyond bearing, she swung round on him. "Listen . . . no, just you listen to *me* for a change, Gareth Sinclair," she insisted as he opened his mouth to speak. "Sam's a nice man, a caring and honest man. He's my friend as well as my employer and I trust him completely."

"I'm glad to hear it."

"And I've never made love with him or with anyone else come to that—"

"Really?"

"—but he has asked me to go away on holiday with him once this *Charlotte Dreaming* business has been dealt with, and I am very happy about that," Morrin finished with a great show of bravado.

"Ah!" He put a lot of meaning into that one syllable.

"What do you mean, 'Ah'?"

"I mean that I'm right. Sam Kennedy is after one thing, and he's about to get it served up on a plate."

"Not at all. Sam has made it quite clear that I call the shots. If I want separate rooms then we'll have separate rooms. Must you always judge everyone else by your own standards?" she asked scathingly.

"My own . . . ?" He glared down at her for a few seconds, then turned and began to stamp back towards the cable car. The air carried his words back to her. "Ye Gods . . . what's an infant like that doing away from her mother? Does she really think that any man worth his salt is going to take her on a separate-rooms holiday?" he asked the sky.

"I'm not entirely naïve, you know!" she yelled after him. The misery and humiliation and self-hatred Gareth had wakened in her, her guilt over lying to Sam, all rose to the surface. She ran after Gareth, slipping and floundering on the snowy rocks. "And I didn't say I wanted separate rooms, either," she panted when she caught up with him. "Sam's a normal man and I don't expect him to treat me like something too precious to touch. But he's loyal and honest and—"

Gareth turned. "Next thing, you'll be telling me that

146

you expect to hear the sound of wedding bells," he jeered.

"Just because you'd die rather than think of marriage . . ." She stopped, baffled, as he started to laugh, peals of mirth soaring up into the clear sky.

"Sweetheart, you don't think a man like Sam Kennedy's going to tie himself down just like that, do you?" he asked when the laughter had begun to subside. "For one thing, what's Vicki going to say about it?"

"It has nothing to do with Vicki!"

"You think not? Come on, Morrin! You're lovely, you're sweet – and from what you've just told me you're virgin territory," Gareth said cruelly, without mincing his words. "He's only offered you this perfect holiday for two to keep you working with me . . . because he wants this play more than anything else, including you."

"He meant it."

"Perhaps he did. Perhaps you're the consolation prize if he doesn't get what he's really after."

"I don't know what you're talking about."

"Don't you? Then you're even more innocent than I thought," Gareth said. "Sam Kennedy really does know a good thing when it comes along."

"You're jealous." The words were out before Morrin even realised that she was thinking them. Don't be an idiot, a small voice told her deep inside her head. Why would Gareth Sinclair be jealous of Sam? And yet she heard herself talking on, the words spilling into the silence between them. "You're jealous because I wouldn't go to bed with you that time in Yorkshire.

147

You're jealous because I trust Sam and I'm willing to go on holiday with him. Because he might be the first . . ."

He caught her by the shoulders, shaking her. "You little fool," he said. "Don't you know why he's paying you all this attention, why he's so keen on me writing this damned play for him? It's not you he wants – it never was you!"

"You don't know anything about me and Sam!"

"You," Gareth said coldly and deliberately, "are a diversion, a titbit to be getting on with. That's—"

He stopped short, releasing her so abruptly that she almost lost her footing on the uneven, snowy ground as a group of people came into view, their voices ringing out in the clear sharp air.

"Shall we get back down to earth again?" he asked, and strode off towards the cable car, leaving her to trail in his wake, miserable and confused, her anger deflated.

The cable-car was crowded during the short journey down. Once, when it jolted, Morrin was thrown off balance, against Gareth. Expressionless, he set her back on her feet, and she fumbled for the rail, moving as far away from him as she could.

She was glad to get back to the car and eager to return to the comparative safety of the villa, and Sam. But by the time they had reached the bottom of the mountains Gareth seemed to have swept their quarrel from his mind, and he insisted on stopping at a small restaurant for dinner.

"You should try some local food, and I'm quite sure

that the others can manage very well without us. Besides, I'm starving," he said, almost plucking Morrin from the car and into the building.

"I've already had local food, the first night we got here."

"That was a restaurant for tourists. This is for locals, entirely different."

He was right, she discovered when she followed him into a plain, small room with white-washed walls and checked cloths on the wooden tables. A group of local people were already there, filling the place with their voices and laughter. Morrin noticed that several of the handsome dark-eyed women looked with more than passing interest at Gareth as he seated himself opposite her at a small corner table.

He ordered for both of them: rabbit stew and potatoes cooked in their jackets and served with a peppery red sauce, plus a bottle of the local wine, red and spicy and just right for the meal. Gareth's earlier manner had changed completely, and throughout the meal he chatted about previous holidays on the island with his brother and sister and parents.

Morrin, sipping her wine and mopping up the last of the sauce on her plate with a thick wedge of bread, felt herself beginning to relax properly for the first time since Sam had dropped his bombshell about reading *Charlotte Dreaming*. She was even beginning to enjoy Gareth's company, she discovered with surprise. She didn't realise that the thought had made her laugh out loud until, pausing in the middle of a story about some mischief he and his sister had once got up to, he asked, "What's so amusing?"

"I was just thinking how much you'd changed."

He raised an eyebrow. "Since you worked for me, you mean?"

"Ssshhh." She put a finger to her lips. "Walls have ears. Sam must not know."

"You're quite right." He poured some wine for her then emptied the bottle into his own glass.

"I meant that you've not been as nice as this to me since we met in London."

"You think so?"

"Come on, Gareth!" She had picked up her glass, and now she waved it at him. "You know the way you've treated me. Sarcastic and teasing, and downright angry. Quite nasty, in fact." She took a gulp of wine.

"Oh, that. I've had a lot on my mind. Sam going on at me, and Vicki sulking, and—"

"—and having to postpone your holiday with Alison."

"That too," he agreed. "And you being determined to keep our previous relationship a secret, as if I was a skeleton in your closet."

"Or a bit of fluff under my carpet," she contributed, and giggled again.

"Exactly. But today, on Teide, then enjoying this meal together, we can be ourselves, without any need to pretend. So I'm more relaxed than I have been since we got here. And so are you. You've stopped being prickly and on the defensive. You've started to treat me like a person, instead of . . ." – he paused, then said with a grin, "a bit of fluff under your carpet."

Just then the Spaniards began to sing, keeping time with the beautiful staccato clapping that only they can do so well. Some of them started dancing on the tiny square of floor available, and Gareth moved to the other side of the table so that he and Morrin could sit together and watch the dancers as they drank their coffee and sipped the brandy he had ordered for them both.

"Come on, let's dance," he said after a while.

"I don't know how to do this kind of dancing."

"You can learn. Just follow me." He pulled Morrin to her feet and she went with him, laughing, on to the tiny dance floor, where they were greeted with flashing smiles.

Time flew by and the little room took on a carnival atmosphere. They kept on dancing, with each other at first, then with strangers, then with each other again, stopping only to sip some more wine and catch their breath.

"Enjoyed yourself?" Gareth asked as they met on the dance floor.

"Tremendously." She beamed up at him. "I don't know when I last had such a lovely evening."

"Good. Unfortunately it has to end. Time I returned you to your Sam."

"Just one more dance," she begged as the music began again, this time to a slower beat.

"One more," he agreed, holding his arms out to her. She slid into his embrace as though they had danced

151

together often. They had, of course . . . but only in her dreams, during the evenings spent in the Yorkshire bedsit a few miles from his grey stone house. Morrin had never guessed then that those dreams would come true in a tiny Spanish tavern, with Gareth in a bronze-coloured shirt and herself in her checked shirt and slacks, her face bare of make-up and her hair a mess.

And yet – she looked up at him as they danced, his dark hair damp with sweat and tousled over his forehead, his green eyes alight with laughter – it seemed to be just right, this moment together, in this place and at this time.

Then the music came to an end and Gareth tilted her face up to his and bent to kiss her, to the resounding applause of their new friends.

"Come on, Cinderella," he said. "Time to go home."

Outside in the cool, dark air, Morrin stumbled and almost fell against Gareth.

"Steady." He put an arm about her. "Try a few deep breaths."

"What did I trip over?"

She was close enough to him to feel the rumble of his laugh vibrate through her side. "A glass too many of that wine, I would say."

"Nonsense, I never drink too much. Anyway," she said haughtily, pulling herself free of him, "that wine was perfectly innc . . . innoc . . . bland."

"Not as bland as you might think. Oops," he said as she took a few sideways steps away from him, like a crab. He reached out and caught her, drawing her back to his side. "And we did have two bottles."

"Two? Are you sure?"

"I'm sure. Come on, we'll walk around a bit before we get into the car. Remember those deep breaths."

Five minutes later she was feeling more steady on her feet, but by the time they got to the car she was beginning to shiver in the cool night air. When Gareth insisted on wrapping his anorak about her she didn't argue, but snuggled gratefully into it as they drove back to the villa. It was too big for her but it was warm and it smelled comfortingly of Gareth. She yawned and eased herself down in her seat, letting the movement of the car lull her.

She didn't realise until her head was on his shoulder that she had angled herself in Gareth's direction. She knew that she should sit up, but the warmth of his body through the soft sweater he had put on was beguiling, and it was almost as though they belonged together, on that lovely, magic night. So she stayed where she was, half dozing, rousing only when he stopped the car.

"Are we back already?"

"Almost."

She sat upright, easing his anorak away from her shoulders. Gareth had halted the car by the beach, where huge waves rolled in, booming and hissing against the black sand.

"I love that sound."

"So do I. That's why I stopped." Gareth leaned across her to roll her window down. Cool salty air enfolded her almost at once. "The sea always makes me realise how

153

important our lives really are in the scale of things," he said quietly.

They sat together in silence for about ten minutes, listening to the waves as they crashed on to the beach then receded, only to come crashing back. Finally Gareth said, "Sam will be wondering if I've spirited you away entirely. I'd better get you back to the villa."

"Wait." She turned, not wanting the moment to end, and went into his arms as though it was the most natural thing in the world. With a wordless murmur he bent to rain butterfly-soft kisses over her forehead and nose and cheekbones before taking her lips in a proper kiss. His mouth, tasting of salt air, shaped and moulded hers just as her wanton body was shaping and moulding itself to merge with his.

Morrin's hands moved of their own accord to the back of his neck, her arms sliding about him to draw him close. She responded when his kiss became more passionate, for he was in control of her destiny now and she could do nothing more to stop him. She no longer wanted to stop him; it was sweet relief to submit, to shut the door on her conscience and let Gareth have his way with her. When his hands eased her sweater back at the neckline so that his mouth could trace a line of molten fire down the soft skin between her ear and her shoulder the touch triggered off a surge of passion that Morrin had never experienced before. She gasped with pleasure and her fingers burrowed beneath his thick sweater to gorge themselves on the smooth, firm skin of his back. Being with him, pleasing him and fulfilling the desperate need he had created in her became the only goals in her world. The past and the future had vanished, and only the present mattered.

Thirteen

When they finally drew slightly away from each other they were both breathless.

"You want me." Gareth's voice was husky with wonder. "You really want me, don't you?"

Morrin couldn't deny it. She reached up to cup his square jawline with one hand, tracing the high cheekbone with the ball of her thumb. Her body felt soft and relaxed, yet more alive than ever before.

He kissed her again, then whispered, "Come out to the guest house tonight."

"What if Sam or Vicki found out?"

"Who cares?" His lips teased their way down her neck to her throat, his hair was soft and springy against her chin and his breath warm on her skin.

"And what if Vicki decides to visit you?"

His chuckle was muffled against her shoulder. "I doubt if she will, after what happened the other night."

A thin thread of jealousy soured the sweetness of her desire. "I know what happened the other night. No need to elab . . ." – she was still having problems with long words – ". . . to tell me."

He lifted his head and starlight picked out the clear green glint of the eyes inches from hers. "You're always jumping to conclusions, aren't you? I told you that Vicki came knocking . . ." As she started to protest he silenced her with a finger on her lips. "I didn't say I welcomed her into my bed, did I?"

"But you must have." She bit down hard on his finger.

"Ouch! You still have a very low opinion of me, don't you? Vicki Queen is simply not my type. I was very tactful about it . . . too tactful, perhaps." He kissed her again. "Now she thinks I'm staying on because I've repented of my hasty behaviour. She's aching to play the part, but she wants me to beg for her favours before she yields. I promise you that I'll lock the door against her . . . once you're on my side of it."

She drew a deep breath, closed her eyes, concentrated on the boom of the waves on the nearby beach. "I've had too much to drink, haven't I?"

"A little too much."

"And now you're trying to take advantage of me."

"Of course." There was amusement in his voice. He was smiling, she knew, but she didn't dare open her eyes. This was a decision she had to make for herself and she could not afford to let the sight of him sway her.

The small practical voice that always came to her at such times warned that Gareth was only interested because she had foolishly told him that nobody had ever made love to her before. Her foreknowledge of his casual attitude towards women fought with her desire.

157

She wanted Gareth Sinclair, wanted the first time to be with him, and only him. Tomorrow, with its guilt and recriminations and, perhaps, its tears, was light years away, and she no longer cared about it.

She opened her eyes, smiled up at him. "Let's go back," she said, and he dropped one final kiss on her nose before switching on the engine.

Neither of them spoke again until Gareth turned the car into the small courtyard before Vicki's villa and killed the engine.

"Oh, hell," he said under his breath, while Morrin looked in dismay at the large car parked alongside Vicki's. The house was well lit and music and the sound of several voices poured from the open windows.

"Did you know that she was holding a party tonight?"

"Nobody mentioned it this morning."

Gareth thumped an angry fist on the dashboard. "Of all the nights to choose! Tell you what, we could just walk quietly round to the guest house. They'd never know we were back."

Common sense began to lay its cold hands on Morrin. "I expect the party's for your benefit . . . and Sam's. He'll be expecting me back." She opened the door and began to get out. "We'll both have to go in and you'll have to mingle."

He caught up with her at the front door, slipping an arm around her. "I don't feel like mingling with anyone but you tonight," he murmured. "You won't forget our own party later?"

As she turned to look up at him he kissed her, his

158

lips swift and hungry. Her blood raced; as if she could ever forget!

"I won't."

"Just in case the address slips your mind," Gareth said, and kissed her again.

She was still in his embrace when the porch light went on and the door opened.

"Hello, Sam," Gareth said lightly as Morrin pulled away from him. "Having a party?"

"I've been worried about you." Sam reached out a hand to Morrin, drawing her close, away from Gareth. "Where on earth have you been?"

"We went to pay our respects to Teide."

"You were supposed to be working."

"Yes – for me. And I gave us both the day off to do some preliminary thinking," Gareth said smoothly from behind her.

"You mean you've been on the mountain all this time?"

"We stopped off on the way back for something to eat." Morrin felt that her voice was loud and unreal.

"Have you been drinking, Morrin?"

"She's a big girl now, Sam," Gareth said. "And a free agent too."

"Have you . . . ?" Sam stopped as Vicki appeared at his side. Tonight she wore a deep blue dress, the bodice consisting of little more than two broad straps, and her black hair had been caught at the back of her head then allowed to hang down her straight, slim back. Her eyes were very bright; as though, Morrin thought with a flicker of unease, she was gloating over a secret.

"Where on earth have you been? Sam was worried about you, Morrin. Clucking like a mother hen. I told him, why hire such young women if it makes you fret when they're out of your sight?"

"I was just explaining to Sam that Morrin's old enough to look out for herself," Gareth said easily as they all followed their hostess into the hall.

"You think so?" Sam made it sound like a challenge.

"Gareth, there has been the most amazing coincidence," Vicki gushed on. "When we were in Puerto de la Cruz today Sam and I met my friends the Hardimans . . . lovely people, they have a villa not far from here. And since they have guests staying with them too, and Cynthia Hardiman adores your books, we invited them all over to meet you."

"A nice thought, but I'm not really dressed for a party." Gareth indicated his casual clothing. "So I'll just slip out to the guest house . . ."

"Nonsense, you look wonderful." Vicki linked her arm firmly through his. "In any case, we have a special surprise for you. You must come and see it at once."

He shrugged, then smiled down on her indulgently. "How pleasant, I love surprises. And meeting my readers," he added with a sidelong glance at Morrin.

"I'll just go to my room," she began, but Sam would have none of it.

"I want you to meet these people too," he insisted.

To Morrin's surprise Vicki chimed in with, "Absolutely, we should all enjoy this party."

The hall was dimly lit and small enough for them to be grouped closely together. Neither Sam nor Vicki noticed the way Gareth's free hand brushed against Morrin's, his fingers tightening briefly on hers before being withdrawn. She realised, as she caught sight of herself in a mirror, that he was probably warning her not to look so guilty.

The four of them moved, Vicki and Gareth leading, Sam and Morrin following, to the steps leading down to the lounge, where several people sat chatting. At the sight of them, Morrin, slightly behind Gareth, saw his head go up suddenly and caught his muttered, "Christ!"

Then one of the women in the room had jumped to her feet and come forward, her hands outstretched towards him, her face glowing.

"Gareth! I can't believe it. Fancy meeting up like this, so far from home!"

"Neither can I. Hello, Cass," said Gareth.

It seemed to Morrin that the world, on its usual headlong gallop through the universe, had come to a sudden stop against a large and unexpected brick wall. Later, looking back on that moment, she was sure that she must have gasped or called out but if she did, nobody seemed to notice.

She stopped on the steps, only dimly aware of Sam's hand on her elbow as Gareth, urged on by Vicki, moved down into the room and towards the girl he had greeted as Cass.

"I didn't expect to see you here."

Vicki released his arm and turned so that now she stood by the girl's side. As Morrin followed Sam down the steps she saw that the actress's eyes, fixed on Gareth, were hard and bright and curious, as though the woman scented a story and was keen to see the facts confirmed.

"Isn't it wonderful, the two of us being here, of all places, at the same time?" Cass took Gareth's hands in hers, reaching up to kiss him with easy familiarity, as though, Morrin thought numbly, she had every right. "As if it was meant. I couldn't believe it when Vicki mentioned that you were staying with her, and writing a play for her, too. Why didn't I know anything about this?"

"Because it all happened very suddenly. Anyway, what are you doing on Tenerife?" he wanted to know. "Shouldn't you be terrorising little children in that Welsh classroom of yours?"

"A typical man," Cass told the room in general, putting her arm through his so that he turned with her, close-linked, to face the others. "You never listen to anything I tell you, Gareth. I'm starting a new job next week, so my friend Anna and I decided to tour Spain and take in a quick visit to her aunt and uncle. Unfortunately it's only a very quick visit. If I'd known that you were here . . . Anna, come and meet the man I'm always talking about."

During the flurry of introductions that followed,

Morrin, staying in the background, had time to study Cass, the childhood friend Gareth had grown up with. She was slightly taller than Morrin, tall enough to look good in her simply cut orange midi dress; quite ordinary compared to the strikingly beautiful women Morrin had seen Gareth with during her time as his secretary, but animated and attractive, with a ready smile, bobbed auburn hair and brown eyes. Eyes that scarcely left Gareth's face, Morrin realised, and felt her heart shrink within her. This, Kate had said, was the girl who had loved him for years, and was determined to marry him.

Gareth, his arm now looped casually about Cass's shoulders, brought Morrin into the introductions, but referred to her only as Sam's assistant. At first, aware that the pleasure and magic of the day they had shared was sliding rapidly from her grasp, Morrin assumed that his casual introduction was his way of putting her in her place now that Cass had swept back into his life; but when Sam, with a reproving look at the other man, supplied Morrin's name she realised why Gareth had been so reluctant to do it himself.

Cass, who had shaken hands briefly and was about to turn away from Morrin, hesitated and frowned, turning back. "Have we met before?"

"No, never."

"But your name . . . it's so familiar," the girl said.

"It can't be a proper party if I don't have a drink," Gareth announced. "Give me your glass, Cass, and I'll freshen it up."

"Didn't you once have a secretary called Morrin?"

163

Cass asked in a clear voice, its faint Welsh accent underlying the words. Then, looking from one to the other, "Surely . . . this can't be your Morrin, can it?"

"I wouldn't say she was ever mine, Cass," he drawled, and Morrin noticed with amazement that the corners of his mouth were quivering. Even now, when everything had gone wrong, he found something to smile about. It was clear that although he had tried to keep her name from Cass, Gareth wasn't going to be an ally now that her secret was out.

"But it's the same Morrin? It can't be!"

Gareth shrugged faintly and raised his eyebrows at Morrin, indicating that the next move had to be hers. She took a deep breath and straightened her shoulders.

"As a matter of fact, I did work for Gareth once," she said. "Briefly, a long time ago."

Vicki's sigh was one of pure delight, and her dark eyes sparkled with malicious interest as they flashed between Gareth and Morrin. Her lips parted, but Sam's voice broke in before she could say anything.

"As Morrin says, it was a long time ago. Now that we've all met each other, who wants a fresh drink?"

His grey eyes were fixed on Morrin and despite the light tone of voice there was shock in his gaze, a bewildered hurt that stabbed through her like a spear. She turned away, unable to face him, as he went on with scarcely a pause, "Gareth, what can I get you?"

The next hour dragged by. Vicki looked like the cat who had stolen all the cream, and Sam, after that first hurt look at her, kept well away from Morrin, not even glancing in her direction. Cass, who had pulled Gareth down to sit on the arm of her chair, talked on and on about their shared childhood and their teens, the games of hide and seek, swimming in the local river, playing tennis and attending the village dances near his grandmother's home in Wales. Gareth added the occasional comment, but left it to her to paint the picture of idyllic youth and a relationship that was too strong to break.

At any other time Morrin would have been fascinated to hear the girl talking about Gareth's grandmother, who had helped her husband to create and build up the family business, and who still ruled over her family. But she was too aware of Sam's hurt silence to concentrate on a word the girl said.

Once Gareth glanced at her swiftly, raising one eyebrow slightly, perhaps in apology, perhaps asking what she planned to do next. Realising that Vicki was watching them both closely, she rose and left the room.

In the small shower-room leading off her bedroom she splashed cold water on her flushed face and combed her hair. She would have given anything to be free to stay in the room, but she knew that sooner or later someone – Sam, perhaps, or Vicki – would come looking for her. With a deep sigh, she went back into the hall, and almost bumped into Cass on her way out of the lounge.

"Oh, hullo. I was looking for the bathroom."

"It's just through that archway, on the left."

"Thanks," Cass said then, as Morrin made to walk past her, "I'm glad I've finally met you. Now I can put a face to the name." She leaned back against the wall. "You've been a bit of a mystery to us all."

"I don't see why."

"Don't you?" Cass's brown eyes, so warm when she looked at Gareth, were hard and cold. "Funny," she went on, "you look as though butter wouldn't melt in your mouth. It just shows that appearances can be very deceiving."

"I don't know what you're talking about."

"Don't let's beat around the bush, shall we? You know very well what I—" Cass began, then as Vicki appeared in the hall she stopped abruptly.

"Something wrong?" Vicki asked, her eyes still bright with malice as she looked from one to the other.

"I was just telling Morrin that we should get to know each other better, since we have so much in common."

"Apparently so. I tell you what, why don't we all go to the Epiphany procession on Friday night? I've booked a table for four, but I'm sure that I could change it. It would be such fun," Vicki purred.

"Yes, it would, but unfortunately I'm due on board the cruise ship that afternoon, so I don't have much time." Although Cass was speaking to Vicki, her eyes were fixed on Morrin.

"Cancel the cruise and stay here. I'm sure that Gareth would like that."

"Perhaps I will," Cass said slowly. "If you'll excuse me . . ." She slid past Vicki on her way to the rear of the house.

"You're a dark horse, aren't you?" Vicki put a

beautifully manicured hand on Morrin's arm as she, too, was about to escape. "I get the impression that poor Sam didn't even know that you'd once worked for Gareth." Her eyes were greedy for information. "So what happened to make you turn so secretive about it?"

"Nothing," Morrin said. "Nothing at all," and she blundered away from the other woman, back into the lounge.

It was a relief when Vicki finally announced that she wanted to take everyone to her favourite nightclub. As the others bustled about, fetching jackets and bags, deciding who should go in which car, Morrin found it easy enough to plead exhaustion and bow out of the excursion.

To her surprise, Cass said at once, "But you must come, mustn't she, Gareth? Tell her!"

"It's up to Morrin, surely," Sam told her.

"But I haven't had time to talk to her yet," Cass protested, then to Morrin, her voice honeyed, "We should get to know each other, since we have so much in common."

"You have nothing in common," Gareth said firmly, and swept her out with the others.

"Sam." Morrin managed to delay him as he was following the others out. "I'll explain everything in the morning."

"Will you, Morrin? Can you?" Sam asked, his eyes as hard and cold as grey slate.

"Of course I can. Don't you trust me?"

"I used to," he began.

Then Gareth said from the steps, "Sorry, just popped back to collect Cass's bag. Oh, there it is." He picked it up then turned to survey the two of them. "Am I interrupting something?"

"Nothing at all," Sam said, and ushered him out.

Once in bed Morrin lay staring at the ceiling. It had been the most wonderful day of her life, and at the same time it had been the worst. She had danced in Gareth's arms, kissed him at the beach . . . and betrayed her true feelings to him. She groaned aloud at that recollection.

And all the time she was kissing him, being kissed, promising to spend the night with him, Cass had been nearby, unknown to them both. Or was it unknown to him? Had he changed his mind about staying on because he knew Cass was coming?

Of course he couldn't have known, she thought feverishly. If he had, he would never have asked Morrin to go to him that night. Or would he? Was that his idea of a joke?

Just then knuckles rapped softly on the door and she sat upright in bed, her heart thumping wildly.

Fourteen

"Morrin? It's me. I have to talk to you," Sam said, low-voiced.

"Tomorrow. Go to bed, Sam."

"Tonight," he insisted.

"All right, just give me a minute." Even as Morrin scrambled out of bed, snatching up her dressing-gown and pulling it on over her short nightgown, the door handle turned and he walked into the room, his face drawn and his normally neat hair tousled.

"I didn't expect you back so soon." She tied the belt of the dressing-gown with shaking fingers. She hadn't had time to prepare for this.

"Only me." He shut the door and leaned back against it. "The others are still at the club, having a good time." His voice slurred slightly over some of the words. She had never known Sam to have more than one drink in an evening, but on thinking back she recalled that he had already had two or possibly three before leaving for the nightclub with the others. "I came back because I want to know what the hell's going on between you and Sinclair."

169

"Sit down, Sam. I know I've treated you badly, but—"

"Is it true? Did you once work for him?"

"Yes, it is true."

"When?"

"Before I came to London to work for you." She smoothed the skirt of the dressing-gown nervously.

"And you didn't tell me? What were you trying to hide from me, Morrin?"

"Nothing."

He gave a short laugh. "You worked for the man, you knew him well—"

"Not all that well."

"You were hardly strangers, were you? Yet when you knew that I wanted to meet him, to persuade him to turn his book into a play, you said nothing. Even when you met at the première in London the two of you behaved as though you'd never set eyes on each other before. And you still expect me to believe that you aren't sharing any secrets?" He paused, then, when she said nothing, "You had an affair with him, didn't you?"

"No!"

"What else can it be?"

"Just because I worked for him, it doesn't meant that we were lovers!" she argued. It was like a bad dream . . . first Gareth accusing her of taking Sam as her lover, then Sam making the same suggestion about Gareth.

"No? The man's a real playboy, isn't he? Morrin, if you won't tell me what's going on then I'll have to ask him."

"No, please!" She sat down on the bed, running her hands through her hair. "When we met in London I was the one who made the decision to behave as though we didn't know each other. Gareth went along with it, that's all."

"But why, dammit?"

"Because if you'd known you'd have wanted me to persuade him to write that play for you." Even to her own ears the excuse sounded feeble.

For a long moment Sam stared at her, silent, then he said, "That man you once mentioned . . . the man who hurt you so badly before we met . . . it was Sinclair, wasn't it?"

"Me and Gareth Sinclair?" Morrin gave a short, shaky laugh. "Oh, come on! I'm hardly his type, you must have noticed that."

"You're not his type, you don't like him, and yet this morning you went off with him for the entire day. You didn't leave a message; I had no idea where you were."

"I thought we would be back much earlier than we were. Maria must have known," she offered. "She loaned me a pair of boots for the snow on Teide."

"So I'm supposed to rely on the hired help to let me know where you are? Why on earth did you go with him in the first place?"

"Because you told me to keep an eye on him. He said he needed time to think about the play," she plunged on. "Would you have preferred it if I had stayed here and left him to go off on his own?"

"He had no intention of writing the play before he met you in London," Sam said slowly. "Did he change his mind just so that he could see you again?"

"Of course not, it's just the way he is . . . I never knew where I stood with him when I worked for him. Whatever the reason, you can be certain that it had nothing to do with me."

"But why did he go along with the charade and pretend that he didn't know you?"

"It amused him, that's all."

Disbelief was written all over Sam's face. He left the door and came across the small room to stand over her. "I'd have to be very stupid to swallow that one. You kept leaving that book around the office and around your flat so that I'd get interested in it, didn't you? And when I opened the door tonight the two of you looked very friendly."

"We had an enjoyable day. Gareth can be good company when he's in the right mood."

"Is that all? You looked radiant, Morrin. Radiant." He sat down on the bed beside her and said with a sudden catch in his voice, "You still do."

"It's the cold air on Teide. I've spent most of the day walking in the snow. Have you ever been up there, Sam? It's like another world."

"I know. I've been looking forward to taking you, once Sinclair cleared off. I'd wanted to be the first to take you. The first—"

There was something about the look in his eyes that made Morrin uneasy. "What about a coffee?" she began, rising to her feet. "I know that I could do with—"

Whether he lost his balance or whether his next move was deliberate she didn't know, but before she realised what was happening Sam had pulled her back down and into his arms, and was claiming her mouth with his.

"Sam, for goodness' sake," she said breathlessly when he eased his hold on her.

"Where's the harm in a friendly kiss? We've done it before and you haven't objected. I expect you and Sinclair kissed when you worked for him. No doubt he kissed you today, when the two of you were out together?" Sam's arms tightened again, his weight against her, forcing her backwards across the bed. "Did he, Morrin?" His breath smelled strongly of drink. "And did you like it?"

"Sam, stop it!" She struggled to get up. "You're being ridiculous!"

"Of course you liked it, you're a warm-blooded female, aren't you? You never object when I kiss you, do you? And I enjoy kissing you, Morrin, very much." He bent his head to hers.

Morrin began to feel fear taking hold of her as she realised that there was nobody to hear her if she called for help. Vicki and Gareth were out, Maria and Jaime were in their own cottage. Pinned helplessly to the bed with Sam covering her face with kisses, she remembered the way she had argued with Gareth when he jeered at her belief in Sam's honourable intentions. No wonder he had found her naïve and amusing.

When Sam tugged at her dressing-gown, dragging it

back from one shoulder, she hit back at him, frightened sobs rising into her throat.

Then the weight was lifted from her and Sam's fingers, gentle now, took her chin, turning her to face him. "Morrin?" The drunken anger had gone and his grey eyes were clear again. "You . . . you're afraid of me!" he said, and when she stayed where she was, unable to trust her voice, he got up.

"Oh God, Morrin, I'm sorry," he said, and blundered out, leaving her alone.

Her first impulse was to jam a chair beneath the door and stay in her room until morning, but the anguish in Sam's voice before he fled from the room could not be ignored. She washed her face, dressed in slacks and a sweater and went to look for him. He was in the kitchen, huddled over a cup of coffee.

"Are you all right, Sam?"

"Shouldn't I be asking you that?" He glanced up at her, then looked away again in shame. "I'm a complete idiot, Morrin. You know that I never take more than one drink. And now you know why. Not that I was ever an alcoholic, far from it, but I stopped after the first when I realised that I tended to behave like a fool when I'd had too many. Darling, I am so sorry."

Morrin found a mug on the shelf, poured coffee for herself. "It's over and forgotten."

"To behave like that to you, of all people. After what happened to you before . . ."

"Sam, please, it's all right. Let's just forget about it."

She was terrified that he was going to start questioning her about Gareth again.

"You're right, of course. I'd better go to bed before I say or do anything else to embarrass us both." He got up to put his empty mug on the draining board, brushing past her on his way there. For a moment she froze, unsure of him. But he put his mug down, paused, said, "Goodnight, Morrin. Sleep well," and left her on her own.

Morrin finished her coffee after Sam had gone, then rinsed the two mugs and put them on the draining board. The front door opened as she was about to leave the kitchen and she tensed, half hoping that it might be Gareth but half afraid to face him after all that had happened in the past few hours.

Vicki slammed into the kitchen, her lovely face twisted with irritation. "Oh, it's only you. Where's Sam?"

"He's just gone to bed. I don't think he should be disturbed," Morrin said swiftly as the other woman turned towards the door.

"Really?" The actress looked her up and down, her eyes blazing. "And why not?"

"He isn't feeling very well."

"He's not—" Vicki began, then stopped short. "He's had too much to drink, hasn't he?"

"You know about that?"

"My dear girl," the older woman said condescendingly, dropping into the chair Sam had just vacated and taking out a cigarette case, "Sam and I go back a long way. We know everything there is to know about each other. Hasn't he told you about us?"

175

"I know that you were drama students together, that's all."

"And best friends, and . . ." Vicki looked up at Morrin from beneath her long thick eyelashes. "Any coffee? It was me who realised that the poor love couldn't hold his drink well, and advised him to stop after the first," she went on as Morrin fetched a cup. "Does he still do that?"

"Yes, usually."

Vicki lit her cigarette. "We always looked out for each other, Sam and me." Her eyes softened in a way Morrin had never seen before and she gazed at the wall, obviously seeing far beyond it. "He wasn't much of an actor and once he realised that and decided to go in for production instead, he promised that one day he would find the perfect play and make me a West End star."

"Did he?"

Vicki snapped back to the present. "By the time he got around to it I was already a star, darling. And we were all grown up by then anyway. So . . ." Her gaze was hard again as it raked over Morrin, taking in the plain dressing-gown, the tousled hair. "You're all on your own tonight?"

"Yes."

"And having a dreary evening."

"I don't mind my own company."

"That's just as well," Vicki said with silky spite, "since you probably get a lot of it." Then, stubbing her partially smoked cigarette out viciously in the ashtray Morrin had put on the table, "I've had a miserable time! First

Sam walks out on me, then Gareth and Cass vanish, leaving me stuck with the Hardimans and that niece of theirs." She accepted the coffee without thanks. "I doubt if Gareth will be back tonight; Cass had quite a firm grip of his arm the last time I saw them." Then she added with mock regret, "Oh dear, I hope that doesn't upset you."

"Why should it?"

"I was thinking about Cass's little surprise tonight. Why keep your relationship with Gareth such a secret? It's my guess that you fell for your boss, darling, and since he didn't return your feelings, you threw up the job."

"Nothing as interesting, I'm afraid." Morrin glanced at the kitchen clock. "If you don't mind, I think I'll go to—"

"And then there was Sam. Lucky you, moving from one gorgeous man to another. I'm surprised that you let him go off to his room tonight when you had the house to yourself. Not" – her eyes swept over Morrin again – "that you're exactly dressed to please any man. You have a lot to learn."

"I don't know what you're talking about."

"No need to be so prim and proper, sweetie, there's nobody else around to hear us. You fancy Sam, don't you?"

"I work for him, that's all." Why, Morrin thought wearily, did everyone seem to feel the need to link her with someone else?

Vicki blew out a lazy cloud of cigarette smoke. "I

hope that's all there is to it. It's never wise to go out of one's depth, if you know what I mean."

"No, Vicki, I don't know what you mean. Perhaps you could explain it to me."

"What I mean is, I've seen better acts than yours in third-rate theatres." Now that they were alone, with no onlookers around, Vicki allowed her full mouth to take on an ugly square look, while her eyes glittered spitefully. "Sam might fall for it, but I don't. You want him, and you've been making it embarrassingly obvious."

With her red-lipsticked mouth, she looked like a malicious pillar box, Morrin thought, and had to bite back a hysterical giggle at the mental picture she had conjured up. Instead she took a deep breath and managed to say levelly, "You're quite wrong."

"I'm glad to hear it, because let me tell you right now, I've no intention of standing by and watching him being snapped up by a little gold-digger."

"Are you telling me that you want him?"

"I'm telling you that if at any time I do, I have more claim to him than you have. So back off!"

"I'm sure that if he could hear you . . . and see you . . . right now he would find this little scene very interesting."

"Not as interesting as the scene we all saw earlier tonight, when we found out about you and Gareth," the actress drawled. She tasted her coffee, made a face, and got up to toss the contents of the cup into the sink. "You've put sugar in this!"

"I thought," Morrin said through gritted teeth, "that

178

you could do with some sweetening." Then, head high, she stalked to the door without a backward glance at her tormentor. Once out in the hall, she fled to the safety of her room.

She should have known better than to court disaster for a second time, Morrin thought as she got back into bed. She should have been honest with Sam from the beginning, and refused to see Gareth again. She should certainly never have allowed her hunger for him to throw her back into his arms. She should have had the sense to know that as far as Gareth Sinclair was concerned she could only be hurt again. And the second hurt was more painful than the first.

Yes, it served her right; but that didn't stop the tears of self-pity that slid from beneath her closed lids as she lay alone in the darkness.

"You didn't come to the guest house last night," Gareth said.

Morrin stared at him, completely taken aback, and dismayed to find him breakfasting on his own out on the patio. He must have come straight from the pool, for his blue swimming briefs were still dark with water and his wet hair gleamed in the sunlight.

"I assumed that you had made other arrangements." She stopped short as Maria appeared from the house, carrying a tray of fresh coffee and rolls. When she returned to the house Gareth asked, "What other arrangements?"

"With Cass. I understand that you left the nightclub together last night."

"Checking up on me, were you? I don't go back on my word, Morrin. You're the one who changed your mind."

She stared at him. "I did what?"

"When you called Sam back, as we were all leaving. It didn't take much to guess what you were saying. He couldn't wait to leave us and rush back here. Tell me, what story did you come up with? I should know, so that our stories tally."

"I did not ask Sam to come back here last night."

"But he did, didn't he?"

"Yes, but—"

"The important thing is that we had an agreement and as far as I'm concerned it still stands."

"Gareth, last night we weren't being serious."

He raised a lazy eyebrow. "Weren't we? You've walked out on me twice, Morrin, and I don't let women do that a second—"

Voices from the lounge warned them that Sam and Maria were close by. Gareth tore open a crisp roll and began to butter it as Sam came on to the patio.

"Good morning," Gareth greeted him blandly. "I was just telling Morrin that with any luck we'll finish the rough draft of the first act today."

"Don't you want to spend the day with Cass?" she asked, the name like a stone in her mouth.

"She'd already made other plans, not knowing that I was on the island. We're having dinner together tonight. And tomorrow I'm taking her to visit Teide before she has to go on board the boat."

"Twice in one week?" Morrin asked sweetly, and he smiled down at her.

"I'll see it through different eyes this time."

An hour later she waited in the guest house, fingers on the keys, for him to start dictating. Instead, he moved to where he could lean against the wall in her line of vision, arms folded.

"Now, where were we . . . and I don't mean in the play, Morrin. I was right about Sam, wasn't I? He's not a white knight ready to die to protect your honour, he's a man like any other man. That's why he asked you to go away with him. He wanted you and last night he got you."

"What did you say?"

"You asked him to come back early and he did . . . to spend the night with you."

"You don't know what you're talking about! You weren't even here last night, you were with Cass."

"You're wrong there. I took Cass home and came back before Vicki did. I heard you and Sam talking in your room."

"Talking, not—" She bit her lip, then said, staring down at her hands on the keyboard, "If you must know, Sam came back to ask me why I hadn't told him the truth about you. He'd had too much to drink and he was – he tried to . . ." She stopped, unable to put it into words, then as Gareth said nothing, she ended lamely, "But he stopped when he realised that he was frightening me."

There was a long silence, during which she kept looking at her hands, then Gareth said, "So now you want me to feel sorry for you because I was right about Sam. When are you going to grow up, Morrin?"

The contempt in his voice stung, and she looked up and into his eyes. "You weren't right! I told you, he'd had too much to drink. He's not good with drink, Vicki told me. Do you have to bring everything down to your level?"

He grinned maddeningly. "My level's real and yours is romantic make-believe. If you want Sam go after him. If you don't want him then let Vicki have him. They suit each other."

"You're so arrogant!"

"And you're pig-headed and stubborn." He picked up his copy of *Charlotte Dreaming*. "You're just like my grandmother . . . obstinate and determined to get your own way."

"So you don't like her very much either."

He stared, his brows knotted. "What makes you think that? And what has my family life to do with you? We were talking about Sam and that childish fantasy you have about him. What do I have to do, Morrin" – he leaned across the table, his face close to hers, his eyes a blaze of emerald fury – "to prove to you that Sam's only after one thing where you're concerned?"

She started to stand up. "You can mind your own business!"

A large, strong hand landed on her shoulder, and forced her back into her seat. "We're here," said Gareth coldly, "to work. So let's get this charade over and done with, shall we?"

* * *

182

Today, Gareth did not need any help. He dictated crisply, swiftly, with only one or two corrections. It was all Morrin could do to follow him, let alone read the words flashing on to the screen before her. It was like old times, when he came to each day's work with the words and scenes already clear in his mind.

Maria brought lunch on a tray, and they worked while they ate, continuing without a break until Gareth said abruptly, "End of scene, end of Act One, and that's it. The first draft of the first act should keep Sam happy for at least a week. And now you're free, Morrin. Free to go your own way."

He tossed the book down on the table she was using as a desk and ran his fingers through his hair, then unbuttoned his shirt and dropped it on to the bed as he went into the bathroom. A few minutes later the shower was turned on.

Fifteen

Morrin started the printer and got up, only then realising that her entire body was stiff after hours of concentrated work. She felt dazed and disorientated. Outside, she saw as she went to the window, the sky had clouded over, hiding the sun, and a breeze had sprung up.

When the printer fell silent she began to stack the pages together neatly, ready for Sam, then gave an irritated sigh as they slipped from her fingers and scattered over the floor. Kneeling to gather them together again she stopped as her eye caught a few words on one of the pages.

"Still here?" Gareth asked when he emerged from the bathroom some time later, bare-chested, his hair filled with drops of water from the shower. He was fastening a pair of light grey trousers. "I thought you'd have rushed back to Sam by now."

"Gareth . . ." Morrin, now sitting on the floor, held up a handful of papers. This isn't *Charlotte Dreaming*.

"It's what Sam and Vicki want."

"But it's . . . it's distorted!" She flipped through the

pages, numb with disbelief. The strength that had made the woman in his book real had been subtly changed to an ability to manipulate. The integrity had changed to a sexual power, the clarity that was Charlotte had given way to someone that was almost unlikeable.

She scrambled to her feet. "It's . . . you can't do this to Charlotte."

Gareth was unmoved. "Your boss wants a play that Vicki can do. I told you that Vicki wasn't Charlotte, but that didn't satisfy any of you. So . . . I've turned Charlotte into the sort of woman Vicki Queen can play."

"But this belittles your Charlotte."

He raised an eyebrow. "I think Sam and Vicki will be quite happy with it."

"What about you? Are you happy with it?"

"It doesn't make much difference to me. As you so sensibly pointed out the other day, the real Charlotte is in my book and the stage Charlotte doesn't matter to me. She'll belong to Sam and to Vicki. That will make Sam happy and that, in turn, will make you happy."

"You mustn't do this!"

He turned from the wardrobe, tossed the dark green shirt he'd just selected on to a chair. "I can do whatever the hell I like. Sam begged me for a play, and I don't even intend to see the damned thing when he turns it into a smash hit . . . as he probably will. Stop nagging, will you? Just be grateful for the fact that you've finally converted me."

"Converted you?"

"That's right." His voice was tight with anger. "I accept that women like Charlotte don't exist any more. They've been replaced by empty-headed, self-centred sex symbols who'll do and say anything to get what they want. That makes life a lot easier for all of us, doesn't it? Now we know where we stand!"

"How can you say such a thing?"

"How can you deny it?" he countered. "Aren't you guilty yourself? The way you hid our relationship from Sam, the way you're swinging from one extreme to the other, teasing one minute and withdrawing the next . . . wanting Sam and yet not really knowing what you want . . ."

Papers fanned again to the floor as he strode forward and caught her up into a fierce embrace that threatened to crush her as though her body was made of glass. His mouth swooped cruelly down on hers in a kiss that seemed to reach into the centre of her being and liquidise every part of her. When he let her go she swayed back. He made no attempt to steady her, but turned away.

"Go away, Morrin," he ordered, and she obeyed, her feet carrying her to the door, through it, and down the steps to the house. Then she was in her room with the door closed, her entire body trembling with reaction.

He was going away tomorrow, she reminded herself again and again. Going back to Alison and Cass and all the other women. And they were all welcome to him.

She herself would never meet up with him again. She would make sure of that.

She paced the room, concentrating her mind on Sam.

He cared about her and she cared for him. She and Sam could be happy together for the rest of their lives.

Gareth went out with Cass that evening. He was not back when Morrin went to bed, and when she met Sam at breakfast the next morning she discovered that Gareth had already eaten and left the house.

"I believe his girlfriend sails away this afternoon, so he wants to spend time with her. Pretty, isn't she? Did you know her well when . . ." – Sam stopped, then said casually, ". . . when you worked for Sinclair?"

"I didn't know her at all. She lives in Wales, near his grandmother's house."

"And you were never there."

"Of course not. I was his secretary, not a friend."

"Good," he said, then, "I've been up half the night reading and re-reading the script. It's good, but it needs changes. Sinclair knows that himself; he says that I can make the necessary alterations since he's new to writing drama."

"Since we've finished working on the play, let's go out today, Sam, just you and me." She needed to get away from the house, needed to be alone with him and to be reassured that everything was going to go back to the way it had been before.

"Sounds great, but I thought that the three of us could work on the play this morning."

"But the first draft's finished and Gareth has gone out with Cass."

"I'm talking about you and me and Vicki, love. After all, she's going to play Charlotte."

"Oh, of course." She had forgotten that in Sam's eyes the writer tended to fade into the background once a play became more than a collection of words on paper. "Later, perhaps."

"Tomorrow. Tonight we're going to Puerto de la Cruz to see the Epiphany procession, but tomorrow will be all ours."

"Epiphany?" Morrin remembered that Vicki had mentioned the procession the night Cass turned up.

"The twelfth day of Christmas. That's the equivalent of Christmas Day on this island. They have a wonderful parade, well worth seeing. The atmosphere's terrific, you'll love it," Sam assured her.

They spent all morning working through the play line by line, speech by speech, page by page. Vicki, in a contrary mood, criticised every single word and action and Morrin, her hand aching from taking pages of notes, marvelled at Sam's patience as he explained, coaxed, cajoled, and compromised.

It became very clear to her after the first hour that Gareth had been correct when he said again and again that Vicki was not the right person to play Charlotte, even the watered-down version he had created especially for her. There was no doubt about her ability as an actress – when Sam persuaded her to go through one of the longer speeches from start to finish without a pause she did it perfectly – but just when it seemed that she had settled into the character, she found fault with something else and reverted to her favourite pesona: Vicki Queen the actress, a shallow and self-centred woman who was nothing like Gareth's Charlotte.

Finally, throwing down the script, she announced that the play was dreadful and she had no intention of ever appearing in it. When Sam tried to placate her she told him that she was exhausted, and if she did not have a massage and get her hair done she would not be in a fit state to enjoy the Epiphany celebrations. Refusing his offer to drive her, she summoned Jaime.

"Does she mean it?" Morrin asked when Vicki had gone.

"No, of course not, it's just her way. She'll come round when she's rested." Sam gave her a tired smile. "Fancy going out for lunch?"

"Yes, as long as you promise that we won't mention *Charlotte Dreaming* or anything to do with it."

"Why d'you think I want to get out of this place? We both need a break and I'm going to make sure that we get it."

"Isn't it great," Sam said contentedly an hour later, "to be off duty?"

"Mmm." Morrin smiled across the table at him. "It's wonderful." They were seated at an outdoor table overlooking silky black sands and placid green sea. Before them lay the remains of an entire fish that, when it was first placed before them, had struck fear into Morrin with its staring eyes and gaping jaws, but had proved to be delicious. Sam had been his old self, and nothing had been said about Gareth and the part he had played in Morrin's past.

"This is what it will be like when we go on holiday together."

"And that will only happen if we can get *Charlotte Dreaming* off the ground." Morrin sat upright. It had been inevitable that they would return to business, so why not now rather than later? "Why does this matter so much to you?" she wanted to know. "There are other plays and other actresses too."

"Not like Vicki."

"She talked last night about the two of you."

"What did she say?" It was Sam's turn to sit up.

"That you were good friends at drama college, and that you used to promise that one day you would put her into a West End play."

A smile softened his face. "Those were wonderful days. No money, but a lot of dreams and plans and ambitions."

"But you never did a play together, did you?"

The smile disappeared. "No, and that's why I want *Charlotte Dreaming* for her. To make up for everything."

"Make up for what?" Morrin wanted to know, but Sam was on his feet, pulling notes from his wallet, hurrying across to pay the bill.

"It's time we went back to get ready for tonight," he said when she caught up with him. "Wait for me in the car, I won't be a minute."

"Sam, what's going on?"

"Nothing. It's personal; you wouldn't understand."

"Try me."

He drew a deep breath. "If you must know, when I began to make my name and my first West End chance came along I broke my word to Vicki and cast another actress in the lead role."

"Why?"

"Because she was better suited for that particular character."

"Vicki told me that by the time you were working in the West End she had already starred there."

"Did she?" A spasm crossed Sam's face, almost as though he was in pain. "She did get the second lead in a fairly mediocre play and it flopped after a week. Then she married and left the profession and that was that."

"Not as far as you were concerned, though."

"No; I felt bad about what had happened. Now I'm in a position to make it up to her. And if I had known that you knew Sinclair—"

He stopped suddenly, and it was left to Morrin to say, "Things would have been easier for you."

"Not to worry." He summoned up a grin and squeezed her arm. "We're getting there and it's all going to be worth it."

"I just want to say that I'm sorry about last night," he said as they drove back to the villa past banana plantations and gardens bright with blossoms.

"I think the lunch said that for you."

191

"I feel like a prat, thinking that you and Sinclair would ever . . . of course you're not his type, not one bit."

"Thank you."

"And I don't mean that you're not good enough for him," Sam hurried on. "I mean that he's not got the sense to recognise someone special when he sees her." He reached over to pat her thigh briefly. "I'm sorry I landed you with him, but it's almost over."

"Yes." Morrin gazed out at the banana plantation they were passing. "It's almost over."

The streets of Santa Cruz were thronged that evening with families in their best holiday clothes, the children bright-eyed with excitement. When they had found somewhere to park the car Vicki tucked her hand possessively under Sam's elbow and led him to the restaurant where she had booked the four of them in for dinner, leaving Morrin to trail behind.

To Vicki's annoyance Gareth's chair remained empty throughout the entire meal.

"He promised me that he would be here," she pouted. "And the boat must be boarded by now."

"I suppose he's stayed on board until the last minute. He'll want to make the most of his time with Cass," Sam suggested.

Morrin glanced at her watch, anxious to change the subject. "Will we be in time to see the procession?"

Vicki nodded to the square. Packed with excited families, it held a huge Christmas tree. "Absolutely, it passes right by this veranda. We'll have a perfect view."

Morrin sat entranced as the procession passed by. Children playing bugles and drums led the way, followed by ranks of girls dressed in red and white and carrying Spanish flags. The three Kings, noble and proud on magnificently bedecked camels, then passed along the narrow street, each surrounded by his slaves bearing gifts and palm fronds.

Caught up in the magic that shone from the eyes of the children, laughing as chubby little hands reached out for the sweets the three Kings tossed to the crowd, Morrin glanced up . . . and found herself looking into cool green eyes that held hers for a long moment.

Even though he was surrounded by a close-packed crowd Gareth seemed to Morrin to stand out, his open-necked white shirt gleaming against the dark night and the rainbow of clothes about him. As she stared across at him he lifted one hand in a light salute, then turned away. Vicki and Sam, watching the procession halt while the Kings descended to bless the children in the crowds about them, had not seen him but as far as Morrin was concerned the magic of the evening had gone. As the last of the procession moved away a breeze touched her bare arm and she shivered.

"Cold?" Sam asked.

"Not really." But she felt, in that moment, that she was being haunted . . . by Gareth, by Cass, by something she could not understand.

"You look a bit drained. Time to get back, perhaps."

"Nonsense!" Vicki said, her eyes alight with excitement. "There's lots to see yet . . . come on, Sam."

193

As she pulled him from the terracing Sam turned to shrug and smile at Morrin, holding out his free hand. She had no option but to take it, and be carried off into the crowd.

For the next half-hour the three of them wandered round the town, stopping finally in a square where excited children played on a huge bouncy castle. In a nearby street there was music and dancing, and before she had time to protest Morrin found herself whisked into a laughing group, away from Vicki and Sam. Laughing herself, dizzy from the noise and the whirling dance, she followed where she was led, forgetting her earlier unease, letting the music carry her feet along and catching glimpses now and again of the other two, who seemed to be enjoying themselves as much as she was.

And then as the music changed a firm hand spun her away from her companions, and she found herself clasped in an embrace that she would have known anywhere.

"You do turn up in the most unexpected places, Morrin of the long hair. Having a good time?" Gareth asked, his arms tightening as she tried to pull away from him. "Let's dance . . ."

For several minutes they moved together in silence, then he said into her ear, "A penny for your thoughts."

"I have no thoughts."

"Not even an opinion?"

"Since you asked, I was wondering if it had been a terrible wrench for you to say goodbye to Cass so soon after meeting her here."

"Indeed it was."

"I thought, from something she said the other night, that she might let the ship go on without her."

"The two of you had a chat, did you?"

"No, just a chance meeting in the hall during the party."

"She did offer but I wouldn't hear of her changing her plans. But forget about Cass, how are you getting on with Sam?"

"Very well."

"You've managed to smooth over the little problem of you lying to him?"

"I didn't lie, I just—"

"Didn't tell the truth," Gareth agreed smoothly. "Has he forgiven you?"

"Yes of course. He knows that he can trust me."

"I never doubted that," Gareth said. "The thing is, can you trust him?"

"Of course I—" His arm tightened, drawing her head against his shoulder, smothering her voice. The crowds all around them seemed to fall away, the noise all about them dulled to a murmur in the hazy background as the two of them danced together under the clear night sky and the old trees filled with coloured lights.

It was like the previous evening, she thought as they moved together in perfect harmony. And then, recalling what else had happened on the previous evening, she drew back sharply when the music stopped and his embrace relaxed. Edging away as the music began again she looked around for the others and was relieved to see that they were coming towards her.

"Gareth, where did you get to? You missed dinner," Vicki accused.

"Cass and I went on board early and had some supper together. We had a lot to talk about. When I left the ship I decided that I might as well come on here. Let's go and have a drink."

"You three go ahead. I think I'll go back to the house. I feel quite tired," Morrin said swiftly. "I'll get a taxi."

"They'll all be far too busy. My car's nearby, I'll drive you back," Gareth said.

"I'll drive Morrin." There was an edge to Sam's voice. "After all, she's my responsibility."

Gareth gave a faint shrug. "So, Vicki, it looks as though you and I are going to be left to our own devices."

"Aren't you coming back with us, Vicki?"

There was more than a touch of amusement in the green glance that moved from Sam to Vicki. "Don't be greedy, Sam," Gareth chided. "You've chosen Morrin, and now I choose Vicki . . . if she's willing, that is."

"Absolutely," she purred, tossing back her long black hair. It shimmered like silk in the lights as she and Gareth, arm in arm, walked into the crowd without a backward glance.

Sixteen

"He's so sure of himself as far as women are concerned," Sam said resentfully two hours later. They had gone back to the villa, made coffee, and were sharing a wide garden lounger on the patio.

"Mmmm?" Morrin stirred against the cushions, reluctant to break the companionable silence between them.

"When his girlfriend sails away he just reaches out a hand and Vicki goes off with him."

Despite all her protestations to Gareth, suspicion was beginning to dawn in Morrin's mind, fanned by Sam's obvious resentment over the way Vicki had disappeared into the crowd with Gareth without a backward glance. "You're not jealous of him and Vicki, are you?"

"Jealous?" Sam dropped a kiss on the end of her nose. "Why should I care about them when I've got you beside me? Have you decided where you want to spend your holiday?"

"Can't we leave that until we get back to London?"

"You haven't changed your mind, have you? We'll have a wonderful time together." He ran the tip of one finger down her bare arm. "You look very beautiful in the moonlight. Remind me to tell you that when we're on some palm-fringed beach together. Or have you decided on some exciting city instead?"

Morrin took a deep breath. "The thing is, I've never gone away with a man before . . . It's different for you!" she added defensively as she heard him laughing in the dusk.

"So you think I'm in the habit of going off with other women?" he teased.

"It has happened, hasn't it?"

"Good grief, darling, I'm not a monk."

"And it's happened with Vicki." Morrin kept her voice steady, her eyes fixed on a distant star.

There was a faint pause before Sam spoke again, lightly. "So? It was a long time ago. We've both moved on since then."

"Yes, you have. *You* got a play in the West End and you didn't give Vicki the lead as you had promised. And *she* . . ." The pieces were beginning to fit together, one clicking into the other. Perhaps it was because she had been working with Gareth on his drama script, perhaps not, but all at once Morrin felt as though she was in a theatre, watching a real-life drama unfolding on a stage. "She gave up the stage and opted for marriage to a rich man instead."

"She threw all that talent away because I broke my promise." A husky note had come into his voice.

"You can't blame yourself for her decisions."

"I knew . . . I know Vicki well. It was my fault. If I had kept my word she might have been a big name by now."

"And you want to make it up to her."

"She's still young, Morrin. She could still do so much."

"You care a great deal for her, don't you, Sam?"

"Why not? We saw each other through some hard times in the past. I owe a lot to Vicki."

"Are you in love with her?"

"What?" He gave an incredulous laugh. "Why should you think that, just because I want to see her succeeding as an actress?"

"Do you love me?"

"Grow up, Morrin; this is the real world, not some teenage romantic fantasy."

"I think I have just grown up. I thought you cared about me."

"Of course I care. Why do you think I want this holiday? It would give us a chance to get to know each other."

She scrambled to her feet and his hand fell away from her elbow. "I don't have to sleep with someone to find out if I like them, Sam. I prefer to do things the other way round."

"It's Sinclair, isn't it? He's turned you against me. Don't you see, Morrin" – Sam was on his feet, reaching out for her – "that he's trying to come between us. He wants you for himself."

She stepped back, away from him. "That's ridiculous. Now, if you don't mind, I'm going to bed . . . alone."

As she turned to leave the patio he pulled her back and into his arms. "Morrin . . ." His voice was muffled in her hair. "You don't understand, do you? I'm not like him. All I want is for you to be happy, for us to be happy. And we can at least do that for each other, for a little while . . ."

His hands spread over her back, tightening to pull her against him, her face pressed against his chest. She could hear the fast thumping of his heart, feel the throb of it against her cheek. She clung to him for a moment, wondering if despite what she had just heard he was, after all, her forbidden flame, that tantalising brilliance that should be avoided, and yet was so desirable. She no longer knew the truth of anything.

He put a hand beneath her chin to tilt her face up to his. His kiss was warm and gentle, and when it was over he eased her away from him. "In that white dress you look like an exotic night-moth." He kissed her again, then bent his head to murmur against her throat, "So beautiful . . . so pure . . ."

Then his mouth was on hers again, but this time the kiss was hard and demanding, his hands greedy and swift, and Morrin began to struggle, knowing that this was not the time, not the way. This was not the man.

Then the two of them fell apart as the patio light flashed on like an accusing eye. Vicki stood in the open glass doors, silhouetted against the dimly lit room at her back.

"Vicki? You're home early."

"Too early." Vicki spoke in a whisper, yet it pierced the night. "How could you, Sam? How could you betray me with this . . . this slip of a girl? This nobody!"

Her voice rose on the final word and she turned sharply and disappeared into the house,

"Vicki?" Sam's voice cracked with disbelief. "Vicki!"

"You're a surprisingly poor judge of women, Kennedy," Gareth said as he emerged from the French windows, his white shirt glimmering in the darkness. "She's been on edge ever since you left us. She couldn't wait to get back to you, and what does she—"

"Get out of my way!" Sam pushed the other man aside and ran into the house, calling Vicki's name.

"So now you know, sweetheart," Gareth said, and then as a car door slammed at the front of the house and an engine roared into life he clapped a hand to his trouser pocket. "Oh damn!" he said, and headed off through the house with Morrin in pursuit.

She caught up with him at the open front door, just in time to see Vicki's car turning out of the courtyard and on to the road. As it roared away the low sports car Gareth had hired reversed then headed in its turn for the road. As it turned Morrin glimpsed Sam crouched over the wheel, his face white and tense.

"When," Gareth said, "will I start remembering to take the keys out of the ignition? It's living in the country that does it."

"Sam!" Morrin ran after the car, then stopped when she realised the futility of it. "What's happening?" She turned to Gareth, still on the steps.

He shrugged. "Vicki was like a hen on a hot griddle after Sam went off with you. She couldn't wait to get

201

back here to see what he was up to. And guess what he was up to?"

"We weren't—"

"She's crazy about him." Gareth cut across the feeble denial as though he had not even heard it. "Haven't you realised that yet? Everything she's done and said since we got here, all her flirting with me and her jibes at you, was her way of trying to make Sam jealous. Why else do you think he wanted me to dramatise *Charlotte Dreaming*?" He came down the three steps towards her. "It was because he found out that her marriage was over and there was a second chance for him. It was never the play he wanted; it was Vicki."

"You're wrong." But even as she said it she knew that he was quite right. She also knew that the last time they had stood together in that very spot, the night they came back from Teide, he had kissed her.

The growl of the sports car engine had faded into the darkness and now there was no sound apart from the sighing bushes and the waves hammering the beach across the road.

"Come inside. We have things to talk about," Gareth said, and Morrin suddenly realised that with Sam and Vicki gone they were quite alone.

"I'm . . . I'm going for a walk."

"We can talk while we walk."

"I mean, alone."

"Not at this time of night," Gareth said. "We've just lost two people, and I don't intend to lose a third. Will you be warm enough?"

"My jacket's in the hall."

"OK." As he went back into the house Morrin seized her chance and ran across the empty courtyard then on to and across the road.

Once she was on the beach the fresh wind from the sea tangled her full skirt around her legs and sand caught at her high-heeled sandals, dragging them from her feet. She let them go, not wanting to waste time retrieving them. The wind had brought clouds with it, hiding the moon and stars, and she did not realise how close she was to the sea until she splashed into the first wave, gasping at its sudden chill.

"Morrin, for pity's sake what are you up to now?" Gareth asked from a few yards away. She turned, and saw him pause on the dry sand just beyond the line of creamy spray from the breaking wavelets.

"Go back to the house. I just want to be on my own for a while."

Fortunately the beach was sheltered from the open sea at that point by a long high rocky barrier that broke the full force of the big waves crashing in from the Atlantic. But even so the wind was strong enough to whip Morrin's hair about her face as she backed further into the water, away from Gareth. She was gasping for breath after her flight, and her heart hammered against her ribs.

"You'd better get out of the water, Morrin."

"I'll come out when you go away."

"I can't just leave you here on your own." Gareth's hands reached out to her. "Morrin . . ."

For a moment the moon broke through the clouds and

she saw to her surprise that he was grinning broadly. "Morrin, I think you should turn round very carefully and have a look at what's behind you," he suggested.

"Behind me?" Without thinking she did as he said, turning in time to see that a huge swell of water had rounded the rocky barrier and was advancing swiftly, menacingly, towards her.

Even as she screamed and tried to run to safety, hampered by her skirt and by the few inches of water round her feet, the swell seemed to rear up to eye level, then higher until it was towering over her, its foaming white crest breaking, curling over, reaching for her greedily.

"Gareth!" She screamed his name at the top of her voice.

"Hang on," she heard him shout, then he was by her side just as the wave hit her, knocking her from her feet. She opened her mouth to scream again, then gasped and choked on a mouthful of cold salty water. Her legs kicked against the wet weight of her skirt and only Gareth's arms saved her from being dragged into the deeper water of the bay along with the wave as it ebbed back, leaving the two of them soaked to the skin, but on their feet.

"You idiot," Gareth said, water sluicing from his tangled black hair and into Morrin's eyes as she blinked up at him. "You stubborn little mule you. You . . . what am I going to do with you, Morrin?" Then, answering his own question. "Let's start with this."

They stood for a long moment in the swirling surf, locked in each other's arms, and when the kiss finally ended Gareth swept her up into his arms.

"I can walk," she protested as he strode along the beach.

"I know, I've seen you do it. And you can run too, but I'm tired of chasing after you, so stay put," he ordered, and for once, exhausted and still shaking with fear, she did not argue.

Seventeen

Ignoring Morrin's protests, Gareth carried her through the house, past her own bedroom door and out on to the patio. In the guest house he dropped her on to the bed, shut the door, and switched on a bedside lamp, then went into the bathroom to reappear almost immediately with his red bathrobe and a large towel. Before she realised what was happening Morrin had been whisked to her feet and Gareth was unfastening her dress with practised dexterity.

"What are you doing?" she squeaked as the dress was peeled off and tossed into a corner of the room.

"Saving you from pneumonia." He unfastened her bra and began to towel her back. "Then we have some talking to do."

"What about?" His touch, his closeness, was setting her skin on fire.

"About us, of cour—" He suppressed a sneeze, then stood up and draped the towel about her shoulders. "But first I'd better get dried myself. Back in a minute."

Once he was in the bathroom she dried herself swiftly and pulled the dressing-gown on then tiptoed across to the door. She had just put the tips of her fingers on the door knob when he said from just behind her, "I must say that that robe has never looked as good on me as it does on you."

She whirled round, startled, to see him eyeing her admiringly from head to toe. He himself was wearing a blue and white striped towelling robe that reached half-way down his muscular brown thighs. "Going out?"

"I'm going to my room."

"You really should have a hot drink right now. Why don't you just sit down and let me make you one?"

"I can do that in the house."

He shrugged. "OK, if you must rush back to your own bedroom go ahead. I'll bring the drinks along in a minute."

"Don't bother, I'll stay for a little while." Realising that she was not going to get away from him that easily, Morrin sat in the chair by the table she had used as a desk and watched as he switched on the electric kettle, then spooned cocoa powder into two cups and added sugar.

"I don't take sugar."

"You do tonight. It's for the shock." He put two large spoonfuls into each cup.

"I'm not suffering from shock."

"You probably will be, later on," he said blandly. "Now then, what are we going to do about you now that you're out of a job?" Then, as she raised her eyebrows, "You don't think that Vicki will let Sam keep you on, do you?"

"Did you mean what you said about them, Gareth? Are they really in love?"

"Believe me, they are. They always were. I tried to warn you, but you're not very good at picking up clues, are you?"

"I'm not as experienced in these things as you are."

"No, thank goodness," he agreed. "That's why I had to keep hanging around here, to pick up the pieces when it all went wrong for you."

"I'm quite capable of picking myself up, thank you."

"You weren't capable of it tonight when the Atlantic tried to claim you as its own," he pointed out, then as the kettle boiled he turned his attention to making the drinks with practised ease. The way he did everything, she thought, watching his deft hands.

"Here." He brought a cup over to her, putting it into her hands and wrapping her fingers about it as though she was a child. The small, unexpected act of kindness brought a sudden surge of weak tears to her eyes, and as she bent over the cup to hide them the steam warmed her face.

A clean handkerchief swam into view through the blur of steam and tears. "Here," Gareth said from above her bent head. "If you're going to cry over Kennedy best to get it done with here and now."

"I'm not crying over him!" She swatted the handkerchief aside and scrubbed at her eyes with the knuckles of one hand. "I'm not crying at all!"

"Not even over your own future? You do realise that you're probably out of a job . . . again."

"I can find another."

"You could come back to work for me."

"No I couldn't, you've already got a secretary."

"I could probably fit you in somewhere. A personal assistant, perhaps?"

Anger drove the tears away. She glared up at him. "Keeping your diary, dealing with phone calls from your lady friends? I don't think so."

He was leaning back against the small table, sipping at his drink. "There aren't any lady friends now," he said.

"There's Cass." Morrin recalled the girl's unexpected venom when they met briefly in the hall. "I don't think she would want you to employ me again."

"Cass has nothing to do with my work."

"She will have when you marry her."

His eyebrows shot up. "Marry her? Is this another bee you've found in your bonnet?"

"Your sister told me, just before I left Yorkshire."

"Kate said . . . ?" Gareth slammed his half-empty mug down on the table. "Why," he asked, exasperation in his voice, "can't women stop matchmaking? Of course I'm not going to marry Cass, that's just some romantic nonsense that the silly girl dreamed up . . . with, I might add, my grandmother's connivance. You know the sort of silly stuff some women come away with."

"But you must have known that Cass was coming to Tenerife."

"Why should I? I only see her when I visit the

family in Wales. Cass is like a sister to me; I've never considered her as anything else. Drink your cocoa."

Morrin took a sip from the cup; the cocoa was comfortingly hot, but far too sweet. "I thought that that was why you decided to come to the island, because you knew that Cass was going to arrive."

"If I had known, I would never have come. Oh Morrin, sometimes I despair of you! I came here because of you . . . because for one thing I wanted to know why you had kept me a secret, like something nasty you had found in your attic or in the shed at the bottom of your garden, and for another I knew as soon as I saw you and Kennedy together that he was too streetwise for the likes of you. I came to Tenerife because I could see that you needed someone to look out for you. And I stayed because as soon as I saw Sam and Vicki together I realised what was going on between them and I didn't want you to get hurt. I really did think then," he said quietly, "that you were lovers. And I knew that if Vicki had her way it wouldn't last."

"We were never . . ." she began, suddenly so tired that she could scarcely bear it.

"I know, I know. But I didn't know then."

"And now you're leaving, going back to England." In a few short hours, she thought. Leaving her to face Sam and Vicki alone when they came back. If they came back.

Gareth set down his cup and went to the window, staring out into the dark night for a few minutes before closing the curtains. "I decided to leave because I wasn't

getting anywhere with you. You wouldn't listen to me."
He swung round, hands tucked into the belt of his robe.
"But now you know everything."

"Not quite. Gareth, is Charlotte based on Cass?"

He gave her one of his exasperated looks. "Of course
not! Charlotte's a mature woman, Cass is still a bit of
a child, like you."

"But Charlotte's real."

"Yes."

"And you care about her."

"Oh yes, I care. More than she deserves at times,"
Gareth said, then, "So what's the next move?"

"I suppose I'd better go home as soon as I can get
a flight back."

"That's tomorrow morning, then. I booked two seats,
just in case," he went on as she stared up at him.

She stood up and put her cup on the table, glaring at
him. "You're always one step ahead, aren't you?" She
pushed her damp hair back from her forehead. "What
is it like, Gareth, being such a perfect human being?"

"It's lonely. Don't go," he said as she moved towards
the door.

"I'm very tired."

He shrugged and went ahead of her to open the door.
Then he paused, his hand on the handle.

"We never did spend that night together, although
we got close to it in Yorkshire."

"As close as we ever will."

"Oh, I intend to get much closer than that," said
Gareth softly. He turned to face her, leaning back

against the panels with arms folded, smiling down at her with a wicked emerald light in his eyes.

"Gareth, I'm going to my—"

He laughed aloud. "It's no use, Morrin, even you can't be taken seriously when you haven't got any proper clothes on," he said, and gathered her into his arms.

"Gareth," she said weakly. "Let me go."

"Typical," he said into her ear, his lips tickling the lobe. "You let me risk my life to save you, then you walk out on me. Will this change your mind?"

He tipped her face up to his and brushed her lips gently with his own. A tremor ran through her body at the contact.

"I have to go back to my room!"

He took a tendril of her damp hair and twisted it round one finger. "All right then, would you change your mind about leaving if I said please, Morrin, please marry me?"

"Gareth," she began, then, in hushed tones, "Did you just say . . . ?"

"I think I just did. You see what you've done? I came to this island a carefree bachelor, and now I'm throwing it all away on a hothead who disagrees with every word I utter. I must be mad."

"You are mad. You can't possibly mean . . . !"

"Oh, shut up," Gareth said, and stopped her mouth with a kiss so long and so passionate that when it finally ended they were both breathless.

"You haven't given me your answer yet," he said huskily.

"But – what about Charlotte?"

"She'll be thrilled once she meets you," he said soothingly, easing her away from the door. "She's been on at me since I was a callow youth to marry someone with brains, someone who could work for a living instead of just using her looks to earn a fortune. Someone like Cass, you see." Then he began to laugh. "My poor darling, you don't understand a word I'm saying, do you?"

"I do. It's all beginning to fall into place. Charlotte's your grandmother, isn't she?"

"At last!" Gareth kissed the end of her nose. "Remember the night of the storm?"

"How could I ever forget it?"

"That makes two of us. When I got to Wales the next day Grandmother started on at me again about marrying Cass so that we could provide her with great-grandchildren while she was still alive to enjoy them, and I suddenly found myself telling her that I'd found my own woman, someone every bit as capable as Cass . . . and every bit as determined as Charlotte, too." He laughed against Morrin's neck. "It gave her a shock, I can tell you. It gave me quite a turn too, because it was the first I'd known of it myself. That's when I realised why I hadn't been able to get you out of my mind the whole damned day."

They sank down on to the bed together, his arm about her, her head on his shoulder. "'Bring her here,' said the

213

bossy old bat. 'Let me see this paragon for myself.' So I hurried home . . . and you'd gone."

When she looked up at him his face was still, his eyes dark green as he remembered. 'I missed you, Morrin . . . you'll never know how much. You were never out of my mind."

"You didn't come looking for me."

"Did you want me to?"

"No," she admitted.

"That's what I figured. I had found you, and frightened you away, all in one stormy night. I thought I had lost my chance, but I never stopped thinking about you, and about Grandmother Charlotte and how incredibly alike the two of you are. And that's when I began to plan *Charlotte Dreaming*. Her book . . . and yours too, in a way. Then . . ."

He kissed her again, then continued, "Then one day there you were in London, all sophisticated and grown up and pretending for some reason that you'd never set eyes on me in your life. And you were Sam's, or so I thought. Lost to me for ever. So . . . I decided to go to Tenerife to teach you a lesson and make your life uncomfortable for a few days and get you out of my system all at the same time. Then when we met up with Vicki I decided that I should stay, just to look out for you."

He paused for another satisfying kiss. "The other day when you stood in the snow on Tiede in borrowed wellingtons and yelled at me like a fishwife, I realised that I couldn't just walk away from you. And I never will. Tomorrow" – he flipped her back on to the bed, leaning over her – "on that plane home to Yorkshire, will be the first day of our new lives."

"But Sam . . ." Morrin put her hands on his chest, holding him back. "I can't let Sam down."

Gareth sighed. "Only you, Morrin of the long hair, could lie in my bed . . ."

"On your bed, not in it!"

"Not quite in it," he conceded, "not yet. As I was saying, only you could lie there looking very desirable in my robe . . . and think about another man. I doubt if Sam cares where you are right now."

"But I care about him. I have to. He went off in a terrible state, Gareth."

"And just a few minutes ago when I looked out of the window I saw him drawing the curtains in Vicki's room. From now on," Gareth said firmly, running a finger very slowly from the soft hollow of her throat to the vee where the lapels of his dressing-gown covered her breasts, "the only man you have to think about is me. And that's going to be a full-time job."

The tip of his finger circled gently, setting up a glow where it touched, a glow that spread swiftly to every part of her body.

"I have to go," Morrin insisted without conviction. "I have to pack . . ."

"Later," Gareth murmured, easing the dressing-gown aside.

His body moved softly against hers, his mouth and hands carrying her to the brink of ecstasy with

215

frightening ease. All at once she stopped worrying about catching the plane; she knew, as his arms tightened about her, that in twenty-four hours they would be in England together, on their way to see Charlotte.

"We have time, my love," he said against her throat. "We have always and forever, you and I."

"Promise?"

"I promise," Gareth said.